A
THUG WORTH
FIGHTING FOR

#1 Essence Bestselling Author

BLAKE KARRINGTON

1

MICAH

*T*he ringing of my phone woke me up from a peaceful sleep. I had just gotten in from a business trip down in Miami at two in the morning and just wanted to sleep the rest of the day away. From my phone ringing back to back, I knew that shit almost impossible now. Reaching over and feeling up on the nightstand, I grabbed my Iphone 11 pro Max, and with one eye open, unlocked it and answered the call.

"Yo Micah, get up man." Hearing my best friend Karma on the other line, I became more alert.

"I'm up, what's good?"

"I just got a call from Kaiser and he said Tracey down there passed the fuk out at one of the houses on Morris Ave. I know you said not to call you anymore wit her shit, but I know you didn't mean it." Tracey was my first love and the mother of my heart beat, Eniko. Right out of College I had promised Tracey the world if she stuck by me and road this journey called life with me. Somewhere along the ride, I never expected to be a single father and for the love of my life to become addicted to coke.

Sitting up in bed, I swiped my hand across my face and sighed deeply. Karma was right about both of his statements. I had specifically told my friends that I was done trying to save Tracey, only for her to constantly submit to that demon that she carried on her back. At the same time I had a soft spot for the person I knew she was before she became addicted to drugs.

I also knew I had to keep the door open for the sake of Eniko. She was eleven years old now and I shielded her from nothing when it came down to Tracey. In this day in age, if you didn't tell your children what was going on in the world, someone in the streets was sure to put them on. For me, education started at home first. That included in the books as well as the streets.

"Man, I don't have the energy for this shit tonight."

"I know bro. I'm headed that way. I can go get her for you and take her over to her folks house."

"Nah, they not fucking with her after the last stunt she pulled. I'm getting up now, come scoop me. I'm so damn tired I know if I get behind the wheel I'm crashing soon as I put my foot on the gas."

"Say less." Disconnecting the call, I threw the plush duvet off my body and sat on the edge of the bed. Flicking on the lamp that sat on my nightstand, the first thing that caught my eye was a picture of Tracey, Eniko, and myself. It was one of the many family photo's Tracey had dragged me to and as always, I made the best out of it. Those were the good ol' days. Tracey and I met on campus my first day at Howard University. She was lost and admiring what she saw. I stepped in, offering my assistance.

"You know, I'm lost too. Maybe if we scour the halls together, we can figure it out. My mama always said, two heads are better than one." I laid my mack down easy.

"Yeah, well she also should've told you not to talk to strangers. Boy move before I'm late to class." She pushed me to the side, straight dubbing me and kept moving about the halls. She would soon learn that I was persistent when I saw something I wanted. I let her go about her day knowing that I'd see her again. And I did, in our economics class, where I sat right next to her.

"And so we meet again. God know what he doing shorty. I suggest you listen to the man upstairs and give me a chance."

"A chance to what? Get me kicked out of this class? Boy, sit back and get yo education." Tracey was feisty and didn't play about her school, I would soon learn. I found that attractive, so I sat back and let her learn. As smart as I was, I could go the whole class without paying attention, but would ace any test put in front of me. I'd always been that way since hell I started school pretty much.

I ran into her again, this time in the hallway. I could tell that she was practically skating to get pass me. I wasn't letting her go that easily. Tracey was a caramel complexioned baddie. Her skin was blemish free with the exception of a small beauty mark above her right eye. Shorty was stacked too, hips on bubble and melons for breasts. Grabbing her arm, slightly turning her around, I spoke.

"Alright, I let you walk away from me the first time. And I let you get through class with no further interruptions. I know for a fact you owe me your number."

"Persistence will get you everywhere." She rattled off her number and switched off. That day I committed the number to memory and from the first time I dialed it, it was on.

It never crossed my mind that the lifestyle I lived would cause the breakdown of my family. I was in the game heavy. No correction; I am the game. It was handed down from my father, Zachariah Hill who had retired a year prior to me graduating High school. I didn't choose the life, and my only other sibling was my sister Macey. Being the only suitable heir to my father's throne, I didn't have a choice. Instantly becoming the boss of all bosses, I let it be known that I would be continuing my education.

I had dreams of owning my own real estate company and without the proper schooling I knew I wouldn't be able to achieve that. So that was the only condition I had when I took over my father's business. Tracey, never knew what I was really into until I told her on the day of our graduation. Up until then, all she knew was that I lived a very comfortable lifestyle. By then, Eniko was already four and Tracey was committed to her new lifestyle.

So committed that she put her dreams of becoming a kindergarten teacher on hold to be a stay at home mom. With much time on her hands it was easy for her to pick up habits. I never thought her favorite habit would be lacing her veins with crack. I can't tell you how much money had gone down the drain for different rehab facilities I'd put her in. The last time I caught up with her, I shoved a picture of Eniko in her face thinking that it would pull on whatever heart strings she had left. It didn't work and in that moment I washed my hands.

Just as I pulled my sweats on, I received a text from Karma letting me know he was outside. It was a good thing that Eniko had stayed the weekend at my dad's house while I went on my overnight trip to Miami. Had I been home, she would've been up wanting to go out with me. Eniko was a daddy's girl at heart. I knew she missed her mother terribly and would express that often by asking questions about her. Eniko was the real reason I kept my line open for whenever Tracey was ready to get herself together.

"Let's hurry up and get this shit over with," I said to Karma as he pulled off. Silence filled the car and the closer we got to the Bronx, the more alert I became. Although I was still in the game, I mostly sat high and looked low. Any movements made, I was the last voice to make the final decision. I rarely showed my face in the hood unless I had to. The fact that Tracey had became a familiar face around the way was fucking with me. Although no one dared to talk shit to my face, I knew for a fact that there was a lot of gossiping happening behind the scenes.

"Bro, you can just sit while I go in there and get her," Karma offered as we made it to the front of the trap. Karma, being my right hand man had played in this exact scene with me plenty of times. He knew that I wasn't going to let him handle my business for me, but he always offered.

"I got it. Text Kaiser and tell him to clear the house. It's bad enough people know who she is. I don't need these motherfuckas all in my face." While I could care less about a rep because I owned the streets, I just wasn't in the mood to be amongst people. A few minutes later, the workers started to file out of the house and disperse. Opening the passenger door, I got out and took long strides toward the building. I mentally prepared for what I would see once I went inside. I ran into Kaiser on my way in.

"She's back there in that room." Kaiser pointed in the direction of the bedroom on my left.

"Who the fuck served her?" my voice boomed throughout the whole house. Kaiser was a killer at heart and had it been anyone else talking to him in such a manner he would've splattered their brain on the cream colored walls. I was the exception though and he knew Tracey was a sensitive subject, so he took no offense.

"Quan did. In his defense though, he didn't know who Tracey was. He was just put on about a week ago. One of the other young boys hit my jack once they noticed her in the corner nodding off." I went to walk away and Kaiser grabbed me by my arm. "She down real bad this time bro. She not even keeping herself up like she used to." Kaiser's tone held empathy.

"I'm already knowing," was my response as I took the few steps to the room where Tracey was. Upon entering, my eyes zoomed in on the figure, crouched down on the ground, appearing to be sleep. The woman before me was a shell of the Tracey I'd known and had come to love. The Juicy couture sweat suit she had on that would've fit her once shapely body now hung off of her like it was two sizes too big. Her hair was in two braids, but the part that split the two was non-existent due to at least two months of new growth. "Get the fuck up," I yelled, not moving from where I was. I feared that if I yanked her up like I wanted to, I'd break something on her.

"Huh?" Tracey's eyes opened and shut as she tried to make out who was yelling at her.

"Get yo' ass up Tracey and let's go."

"Micah?"

"You knew I would come for you didn't you? You know this is my block. Why you keep fucking with me Tracey?" Before I knew it, my earlier thoughts went out the window, and I ran over to her, jacking her up by her hoodie, pulling her up off the floor. "Talk! Why you keep fucking with me?" By now my eyes started to burn because I wanted so bad to cry at the way she flinched when I spoke. This was the woman I loved. A woman I bore a child with and was set to spend the rest of my life with.

"I'm sorry," she whispered with her eyes cast down to the floor. "I'm fucked up Cah baby. There's no helping me. I come here because this is the only way I can be close to you." She leaned into me and I allowed her to rest her forehead against mines.

"You need help Tracey. I can't keep doing this shit with you. Eniko deserves better. I can't be her mother ma."

"She don't need me Cah. I'm too deep in this shit. She has you and that's why I can sleep good at night because I know she has you." Disgusted, I took a step back and took a deep breath to clear the tightening in my chest for what I was about to say.

"If you don't leave here and get cleaned tonight, I'm done. I'm forreal this time Tracey. This shit ends tonight. I will be there every step of the way if you choose us; me and Eniko tonight." I gave the ultimatum and my voice held conviction. A nigga was tired. I could no longer be everything for Tracey that she didn't want to be for herself.

"Micah, I love you and Eniko more than anything in this world, but I can only get clean for me. Right now, baby, I'm just not ready." That was enough for me. She had made her choice and I had to make peace with it. Turning on my heels, I went right back out the door, making a stop at Kaiser before exiting.

"You send a bulletin out to every fucking trap we own from here to Vegas with her picture and tell them not to sell to her. Anyone who does, will be decapitated. After tonight, only call me if you find out she's dead before I do." I made my way back out to the street, heavy hearted knowing that Tracey was right about one thing, she couldn't get clean for me and Eniko. She had to want it for herself.

2

TRACEY

I watched Micah walk out, leaving me alone with my thoughts. In my mind I knew that it was right to follow him, but my heart so desperately wanted to get high. The feeling that crack gave me was unexplainable. Each time I hit the pipe or stuck a needle in my veins, the chances of being back with my family again drifted further and further from my reach. There was no denying that I missed my daughter something terrible and the sight of my first love made my heart rate quicken.

Due to my choices over the last few years, I had come to the conclusion that my now eleven year old daughter more than likely hated me. There was once a time where you wouldn't see me without the her. Eniko was often referred to as my mini me and I carried her as such. Often, I would escape in my mind to a place where things were back to normal, only to be slapped in the face with my harsh reality.

Lifting my body off the wall, I shook my head in attempt to get myself together. Micah had totally fucked up what was left of my high. Seeing him reminded me of who I used to be before my life was turned upside down. Finally standing, my equilibrium was a little off, but I managed to make my way out of the room. I went in search of the young kid that served me the first time, only to run into Kaiser.

"Come on sis, let me get you home." His voice was filled with sympathy, but I could see the hint of disgust in his stare.

"I'm good Kaiser. I got myself here, I can make it back home. I don't need y'all babysitting me." I tried to move pass him, only for him to block my path.

"You know, between me, Cah, and Karma, I'm not going back and forth with you. I'm driving you home and that's that. Whatever you choose to do once you get there is on you." Kaiser went to grab my arm and I snatched it back quickly. Not fazed by my attitude, he moved to the side and let me walk ahead of him. As we walked towards the front door, I made eye contact with the guy from earlier. He quickly looked away, understandably so. I knew Kaiser would fuck him up if he even breathed wrong.

Climbing in the backseat of Kaiser's Acura TL, I made sure to slam the door behind me. I wanted him to know how pissed I was. My high had officially worn off and I wasn't a nice bitch when I needed my fix.

"You need to chill the fuck out. Slamming my door like you ain't got no damn sense. You may be on that shit, but you haven't lost yo damn mind," he scolded me and I laughed.

"Serves his ass right for not letting me get my last hit before taking it in," I thought to myself.

"You hungry?" He asked pulling into a McDonalds drive thru.

I turned my nose up in disgust. I didn't do fast food. Oddly enough, crack was the only bad thing I put into my body. I was on a plant based diet, with the exception of some meats. "You know I don't eat that nasty shit. Stop playing with me."

"Shit, it don't look like you eating much of nothing these days." Sticking my middle finger up, I made sure he could see it in the rearview mirror. I was aware that my clothes hung off of me, but I knew for a fact I wasn't out here looking like a crackhead; at least I didn't see it. There was no need to dispute that fact with Kaiser though. He always gave his opinion raw, uncut with no chaser. Putting my hoody over my head, I rested it against the window.

"Yo T, we here," Kaiser announced once we pulled in front of my building on Morningside Drive. I exited the car with new found excitement, remembering I had a little piece of rock that I'd left on my bathroom sink from the previous night. "Aye," Kaiser called out to me, I stopped, but didn't turn around, "just because you got that monkey on your back don't mean you stop being family T. Eniko misses you and all we want is for you to get clean. You don't gotta fight this shit alone." Feeling emotions that I so desperately tried to detach myself from, I continued walking and didn't respond.

Using my key card, I swiped it on the magnetic pad to get into the building. As always, the weird guy that sat behind the desk in the lobby tried to make small talk. I brushed passed him and made a b line for the elevators. Smashing on the button for the elevator to come down with a sense of urgency, I salivated at the thought of the drug swimming through my veins. The elevator dinged, indicating it had finally reached the lobby.

I pushed my way through the people as they exited and pressed the button for the seventh floor twice. *"Come onnnn,"* I spoke aloud in an impatient tone. It seemed like the elevator knew what I was rushing to and it was taking forever to get me there. The slow ride couldn't prevent the inevitable though. Once the doors opened, I all but skipped to my apartment door. Opening the door, I went straight for my master bathroom.

One look at my apartment, you'd be willing to argue that I wasn't the same woman who was escorted out of a trap house a little while ago. My apartment was immaculate. Not a thing was out of place. The cream colored sectional fit perfectly in my massive living room that overlooked Morningside park. The plush white carpet made you have a conscious when you thought about stepping on it with your shoes on. Although Micah despised my new lifestyle, he still made sure that I lived in nothing less than the best.

Snatching up my pack from the sink, I sat on the bathroom floor against my garden style tub searching my arm for the perfect vein. My arm was full of small track marks that were evidence as to how much of a pro I was at this shit. Finally finding a vein, I stuck the needle in my arm and let the drug do its thing. Throwing my head back, I was ready to embark on the journey to lala land even if it didn't last long.

The next day I awoke to banging on my front door. My eyes opened and noticing that I was still in the bathroom, I laughed hysterically. *"I be fucking trippin',"* I said to myself as I stood to discard the needle. The banging at the door started up again followed by a loud voice.

"Tracey, come open this door before I start acting ignorant out this bitch and wake these white folks up out they peaceful slumber." My cousin Amanda's voice made me sober up real quick. Well, as best as I could.

"I'm coming, damn," I shouted out while making a mad dash to the kitchen to shove the needle deep into the garbage. I wasn't expecting a visit from Amanda, but it wasn't uncommon for her to pop up unannounced.

"Hurry up dammit, I gotta pee." Finally making it to the door, I opened it and Amanda was on the other side with her hand on her hip. "What took you so damn long? You in here getting high?" She put her phone up to my face and the flashlight nearly blinded me.

"Girl, stop playing with me." I slapped the phone out of my face and Amanda flinched at me playfully. "Amanda, get the fuck on. I thought you had to use the bathroom."

"Alright, alright I'm going. When I get out, we need to talk, on some real shit." I shooed her and went into the kitchen to find something to snack on. These days I didn't have an appetite. The dope was all the food I needed. Finding a fruit medley I made the day before, I took that out to munch on. "I hope that ain't all you got to eat in here Tracey." Amanda had returned from the bathroom and headed straight for the fridge.

"Umm, you just came from home right. You should have eaten there."

"And miss the opportunity to eat on some of the expensive shit Micah got you eating? Girl, I think not. Besides all I got is ramen noodles at the house. I ain't go food shopping yet."

"All I have is organic stuff, so knock yourself out." Picking up my bowl full of fruit, I moved towards the living room. Grabbing the remote, I turned the tv on and navigated to Hulu to catch up on Greys Anatomy. I heard rummaging in the kitchen, but didn't bother to turn around to see what Amanda was doing.

"Forreal Tracey?" I heard before turning around to see what Amanda was talking about. Seeing her holding something in her hand, I zoomed in and saw it was the needle from last night. Standing, I marched over to her and snatched it from her hand before throwing it back in the trash.

"So you go through people's trash now? That is so intrusive Amanda." I tried deflecting as opposed to admitting that I hadn't taken the steps to kick my habit.

"Oh, so we not gonna talk about the real problem here?"

"What real problem Amanda? Damn!"

"The fact that you are a functioning addict that won't get her shit together long enough to take care of her damn child!" The words had left Amanda's mouth and she didn't bother taking them back. Instead she stared me down as if she was daring me to deny what she was accusing me of being.

"Get the fuck outta my house Amanda," was all I could come up with. It was one thing to be an addict, but to have your motherhood questioned because of it was another. I knew exactly who I was, and I was well aware that my addiction had cost me more than a little bit. Still, I wasn't ready to part with my favorite pastime.

"Oh, you want me to leave? So you can go shoot some more of that shit up ya veins right. You wanna put yourself out of your misery, do it with me standing here!" I looked at my cousin like she was crazy as she yelled at me in my own home, after being told to leave. "Don't stand there looking stupid. Go get your pack and shoot that shit in your veins with me right here," she dared m. Only, I couldn't. I had no problem with shooting up in front of strangers who were just like me, but to do it in front of a family member was out of the question.

"Just go Amanda. You set out to make me out to be a bad mother and you accomplished that, so you can go now."

"Oh, no boo, you doing a great job of that yourself." Amanda wasn't going to sugarcoat shit for me and I knew it. A straight shooter by nature, her words cut you deep, but I knew that for me, it came from a loving place. "What's it going to take to get you back?"

"Like I told Micah, I have to want it for myself Amanda."

"And what about Eniko? How long is she supposed to wait around for her mother to come back to her?" My eyes welled with tears that I didn't bother trying to wipe as they fell down my face.

"She's doing well without me Amanda, her dad makes sure of that. Y'all have to give me space to make the transition. This shit ain't no easy fight." By now my face was full of tears, making Amanda embrace me. Amanda wanted to fight the battle she felt I was too fragile to fight on my own, but the reality was, she couldn't. I think that was the part that fucked her up every time.

"I love you T and I want what you want deep down inside for yourself; peace. You can't fight this demon alone, but you can't fight if you haven't decided to even step into the ring." With that said, Amanda pulled away, grabbed her bag and walked out of the apartment, leaving me with some food for thought.

3

MICAH

"Daddy, here's the permission slip for the mother daughter tea my school is having next month. I already marked no for the answer. I just need you to sign it." Eniko handed me a paper before sitting down on the opposite side of the kitchen table for breakfast.

"Hold on babygirl, why would you select no? You don't wanna go to the tea?" I asked already knowing the answer, but hoping she felt otherwise.

"Come on dad, you already know the answer to that."

"How bout I ask Amanda if she's off that day then she can take you?"

"She's not my mother and I don't want people asking me questions, its weird and embarrassing. It's bad enough that I have to watch as my friends are picked up from school by their mom's while I'm making up stories as to why mines isn't around." With no further explanation, she poured cereal into her bowl and sat the box in front of her face, so that I wouldn't see her. I was stuck because the older Eniko got, the more things became clearer to her about her mother's addiction. She acted as if it didn't phase her, but I knew my daughter and Tracey's choices were hurting her. Hearing sniffling from the other side of the table, I quickly rushed to her side.

"Don't cry babygirl. I'm sorry, daddy is so sorry he allowed this to happen." I held my broken daughter as she cried for her mother. I wanted so bad to just erase every memory she had of Tracey, but I knew it couldn't be done. Before Tracey got hooked on drugs you would hardly ever see her without Eniko attached to her hip. It was breaking my heart that Eniko was now more aware of her mother's absence and it affected her a great deal.

"Daddy," she spoke while sniffling, "would I be wrong if I said I just want to forget about mommy? That way it won't hurt as bad."

"I wish I had the answer for you Niko, but I don't. I wish I could take your pain away, but I can't. Mommy loves you, she's just in a bad place right now. Drug addiction is hard to shake, and as much as I want to pull her out of this for your sake, I can't." She wiped her face and straightened her shoulders.

"You don't have to make excuses for her daddy. Here, sign the slip for me please because I'm not going." She placed the paper in front of me and walked away. I hung my head in defeat. I could control the streets and businesses I had, but I had no control over this situation. That fact in itself bothered me. Checking my Audemars watch, it showed we had thirty minutes before Eniko had to be to school and I had to be at the office. On top of being the plug, I was the sole owner of both a real estate and trucking company.

While I oversaw and gave clearance before product hit the streets, I spent most of my days in the boardroom. I ran the legit companies just like I ran my drug empire. Putting quality product out on every end. Standing up and pushing the dining room chair under the table, I grabbed the paper and put it in my back pocket. I was gonna make sure Eniko didn't miss out on her event. If that meant I had to escort her myself then so be it.

"I'm ready to go dad. I'll meet you in the car." Eniko was almost towards the door before he stopped her.

"Aye, you know you don't leave out without me. Chill, let me grab my phone." Picking my phone up from the counter, I made sure to set the state of the art alarm system before following her out to the garage. We lived in a secluded area out in Westchester. I didn't have security around my home because I made sure it was locked down like fortknox. To the outside world I was a public figure, as far as my legal businesses went, but I was even bigger on the illegal side of things. It would be a badge of honor for a lame ass nigga if the took out Micah Hill.

I was good everywhere I went. The two glocks I kept on me at all times ensured that. As far as Eniko went, she always had eyes on her whenever she was out of my sight. My babygirl was looked after like Sasha and Malia Obama. I played no games behind my heart. Hitting the locks on my cocaine white Maserati, Niko took her seat on the passenger side. Changing the bluetooth to connect her phone, Justin Bieber's new hit "Yummy" came through the speakers. I had to agree with the masses that the kid was making a comeback with this one. Glancing over at Niko, I watched as she sang along with the lyrics and did little dances in her seat. I loved my daughter something awful and wanted to do whatever I could to keep her smiling.

Making it a point to drive her to school every morning, I tried my best to pick her up every afternoon for the little bonding moments. With her being apart of so many extracurricular activities, I had to buy her a planner just so she could fit me in. The song ended just as her phone started to ring. Pop Pop flashed across the screen. It was my father, Zachariah Hill aka Zack calling her.

"Good morning pop pop," she sang into the phone once it connected.

"Hey, miss lady, on your way to school?"

"You know it. Daddy's right here too."

"Hey pops, what's shaking old man?" I greeted my first ever best friend.

"Nothing much, just calling my favorite girl to see if we were still on for our Friday night bingo down at the senior center."

"You know I'm there grandpa. Ms. Edna owe me $20 for giving

her one of the winning cards last week." I chuckled at Eniko's facial expression. Her and my dad had a bond just like he and I had growing up, if not better.

"And how you knew it was the winning card Niko?" I asked.

"We are one with the cards," she and Pop pop said at the same time, making us all laugh.

"It's a skill daddy. I'm sorry pop pop didn't teach it to you."

"Yeah okay." I let them continue their conversation. It was funny to hear them come up with different strategies to win, which included sitting at a certain table. Pop pop and Eniko together were a trip. "Aight dad, we just made it to the school. I'll have her to you this evening."

"Miss lady," he called her by the nickname he'd given her when she was first born, "did y'all reach the school yet?"

Niko covered her mouth to stifle her giggle. We were a block away from her school, but I knew I had to lie to get my father off the phone. Since my mother and sister had decided to leave him for nearly a year to see the world, he was bored and needed someone to spoil. He now was always tryna hog Eniko and today, I wasn't having it. "Not yet grandpa, we're close though." I tickled her with one hand and she laughed while mouthing, she was sorry.

"I knew it. Son, you are truly a hater. Anyway, Miss lady, I'll see you later. I love y'all and be careful out there Micah."

"Always. Love you too old man." I hung up the call and tickled Niko some more. "You ain't have to snitch me out." We pulled into her school parking lot and Eniko got out before I did, trying to beat me before I could follow her inside.

"My bad daddy," she said still laughing. "Uh uh, remember we agreed that you were no longer walking me inside. My teachers be gawking at you like a steak on the grill. Nope, I'm good. Thanks for the ride dad, love you."

"Now, whose the hater," I yelled out as she ran up the steps to the school. Once I made sure she was inside, I placed a call to her security detail and waited until they arrived before pulling off. My first stop was my office at E Luxury Realty to sit in on a board meeting. Being in real estate was very lucrative if you knew how to run your business. For me, it worked being that I had managerial experience running a drug empire since eighteen.

The homes the company sold were the product, and the realtors were my lieutenants. I ran a tight ship and together, they all made shit happen. Entering the office, my team had already gathered in the boardroom. It was Monday, so new listings were assigned, two per person. Together my team was made up of six people. Four of the six were women and had been in the real estate business prior to me developing the company. The two guys were fresh out of College and I had met them on a trip I took back to Howard. Seeing potential, I paid for both guys to go through real estate courses and obtain their licenses. Now, they were on a level playing field with the best of them.

"Alright, everyone has their assignment. Let's go get this money, meeting adjourned." Everyone stood and went their separate ways. I got up and made my way to my own office. The room was massive and fit for the king I pegged myself to be. I'd hired an interior decorator and told her the vision for the office was the white house; the black one. Not the circus Trump sat in now. Getting comfortable at my desk, I pulled out my cell to send a message to Kaiser. Reading my mind, the phone rang and Kaiser was on the other end of it.

"I was just about to text you. What's good?"

"Let me find out you miss me," Kaiser clowned.

"Man, get outta here with that gay shit. I was reaching out to check on the blocks. Everything moving like it's supposed to?"

"Like a well oiled machine."

"That's what I like to hear."

"Yo, I meant to let you know that I got Tracey home safe the other night. I sat outside her crib for like an hour to make sure she ain't dip off either."

"That's wassup." I was short. I had already explained to both Kaiser and Karma that I didn't want to hear anything else about Tracey. The more I thought about her, the more it made my head hurt. I listened as Kaiser spoke in a coded language, giving me a run down of incoming shipments and monies needing to be picked up. Hearing a knock on the door, I looked up just as my receptionist, Jackie let herself in . As always, she was dressed in some tight shit, with a low cut to entice me.

I wasn't interested in messing around with my employees. Even if I was, Jackie had taken herself out of the running by throwing herself at me. I liked a certain caliber of woman and she didn't make the cut. I ignored her and kept with my conversation. Seeing that I wasn't paying her any mind, she cleared her throat. I set my phone on the table and gave her my attention.

"You need something?" I asked in a voice that should've told her to beat her feet.

"Who that, Jackie thirsty ass?" Kaiser inquired making me laugh. Before I could answer, he called in using face time. I removed my air pod and put him on speaker. "Yeah, I knew that was her. Yo, Jackie, why don't you get a sip of that expensive ass water you be ordering and leave my boy alone. He don't want you ma." Her face flushed red with embarrassment. Sucking her teeth, she left the room without saying anything.

I laughed at Kaiser's ignorant ass. "You cold bro. You hurt that girl feelings."

"Ahh man, her ass ain't got no feelings. I bet a stack she'll be back in your office acting like she working in the next ten minutes." He wasn't lying. Jackie was persistent to say the least.

"Aight man, let me get off this phone. I got work to do."

"Same, I'll check you in a few." After hanging up with Kaiser, I stayed in my office for a few hours to go over listings we had sold within the last month. Pleased with the way the company's bank account was looking, I sent out bonuses a little earlier than usual. I liked to look at my employees as extended family, so I made sure to take care of them. My intercom beeped and again, it was Jackie.

"Yes Jackie."

"You have someone out front requesting to speak with you," she spoke with an attitude.

"Did you get a name?"

"Yep, she said her name is Amanda." I couldn't help but laugh at her pettiness. Amanda had been here on multiple occasions. Jackie knew exactly who she was.

"You can send her back. You're a trip man." Hurricane Amanda stormed into my office with a scowl on her face.

"You betta get that low budget Selena looking ass bitch before I whip her candy ass," Amanda threatened loud enough for Jackie to hear before closing the door behind her.

"Calm down Mandy, what you doing here?" She walked over to me and gave me a brotherly hug before sitting down.

"I went to visit Tracey." I sighed and swiped my hand down my face. This shit was getting old. "We gotta find another way to get through to her Micah. She's not getting it and I'm afraid she's too far gone to reel back in." I agreed with her and didn't know what she wanted me to say. If Tracey couldn't get right for our daughter then it was really nothing else to talk about."

"I offered my assistance and you see where that got me. This time around, I'm letting her figure it out for herself. I have a one track mind and that's making sure Eniko Hill is good. You know she told me she wishes she could forget that Tracey even exists? My baby is in pain and I can't keep putting her through that."

"I know and trust me I hear where you're coming from."

"What you up to Friday night?"

"Shit, Aaron had to go out of town for the weekend, so I'll be home tracking his phone. You know how I do." She spoke as if what she just said was normal.

I chuckled. "You need to stop doing my boy like that. Eniko has a mother daughter dance this Friday and she doesn't wanna go. You think you can convince her?"

"Consider it done. Don't worry, I'll handle it." She stood and hugged me again before walking out. I fucked with Amanda heavy. She had been picking up the slack and making herself available to Eniko whenever she could in Tracey's absence. Shutting my computer down, I left out a few minutes after her. Since I was leaving early, I'd be able to pick Niko up from school. I stopped at Jackie's desk before leaving.

"Aye, I need you to reach out to the temp agency and find me another assistant." I no longer wanted to work closely with her, so because of her unprofessionalism, she was going to help me find her replacement.

4

KELLY

"Ma'am, do you have another card we can use?" The cashier at Whole Foods asked while holding my Chase card out for me to take.

"Another card? That one works just fine. Here, try putting this bag over it," I handed her a plastic bag to put over the card to see if some magic money would appear. "I've been having some trouble with the strip." I knew the card didn't have anything on it, but my overdraft protection was more than enough to cover the $30 worth of items I had on the belt.

"Look, I swiped it twice and there's nothing on the card. Do you have another form of payment?" she snapped at me. I heard the guy behind me call me a bitch under his breath and knew if I didn't walk out the store I would be carted off to jail. I couldn't afford my groceries, so I knew for damn sure that I couldn't afford to bail myself out. The old Kelly would've asked the bad wig wearing ass bitch to step outside, but this new Kelly knew that I was one black out away from killing someone. Snatching my card from the girl, I left the supermarket empty handed.

As soon as I put my hand on the handle of my car, I broke down. This couldn't be life. There's no way I went from top sales associate at a telecommunications company to unemployed and broke. There was never a time where I couldn't afford groceries. My car was the only thing I had left after my ex drained both my checking and savings account right up under my nose. I should've known he wasn't shit from the start by his name; Damien.

Opening my car door, I threw my purse into the passenger seat and banged the steering wheel. "Fuck you Damien," I yelled out before punching the steering wheel multiple times, wishing it was his face. The only reason I still had the Toyota was because I had paid it off. How did I let a man con me out of my ten thousand dollar savings and the couple of hundred I had in my checking account you ask? Well, the answer was quite simple, my ass was DUMB. I bet you thought I was gonna say something about being in love didn't you.

Yeah, no. Love didn't have anything to do with it. I was more so dick silly than anything. I should be ashamed to say that because I was twenty nine when that happened, it is what it is. Damien came into my life when I was on a high. I was at the top of my game at the telecommunication company, had my own place, own car and A1 credit. What could a nigga do for me that my jack rabbit couldn't? Oh, I know, ROB ME.

We met at a club while I was out with my best friend Heaven. Damien's smooth talking, cute ass came over and chatted me up for about thirty minutes before I decided to throw caution to the wind and invite him back to my place. Mistake number one. After I invited him over, he never left. On the outside looking in, it may have seemed like I didn't mind him over staying his welcome, but I did. At first he had a job doing construction and was making good money. Or so I thought. The little dates and just because gifts lasted for a good six months until I met the nigga in him.

He got laid off from his job and started to depend on me. Being the independent woman I'am that was fine because my bills and needs were taken care of. Stupid me gave him access to my accounts, never thinking he'd do no snake shit. I worked and came home to a clean house and food on the table, the roles were reversed and I couldn't see past the fact that he was treating me good. Fast forward six more months and I get laid off because the company I worked for decided they no longer had any use for my department.

Two unemployed people can't do nothing, but fuck, eat and watch tv all day. And that shit got old real quick. While I was looking for jobs, Damien was content with not working. He was content because he was siphoning money from my accounts and doing god knows what with it. I didn't know until I got a call from my bank telling me they had put a hold on my account for too many withdrawals from my savings account. When I inquired about the balance in my account, I almost passed out when she told me the number.

Five hundred fucking dollars was what that bastard left me. Of course he was nowhere to be found when I got the news. His ass had just up and disappeared. I lost my apartment because I could no longer pay the rent and was forced to move back home with my mother. And I'd been there ever since. I was a thirty year old woman, living with her mama. The trip down memory lane was draining. Closing my car door, I drove home.

It was late and I just wanted to lay down and go to sleep. Some days just deserved a do over and this was one of those days. We lived across the street from Grant projects, but with the high traffic every night we might as well have lived in Grant. Parking my car on the corner, I got out and hoped the agitated look on my face prevented anyone from talking to me. Inside, I pressed for the elevator and as I waited, I noticed a guy that I saw at least once a week leaving one of the first floor apartments with a big black duffle bag in his hand. Usually, I would speak, but not today. I turned my head quickly, hoping he didn't catch me looking.

"Aye, you ain't speaking today beautiful?" He said, switching the bag to his other arm.

"Tonight is just not my night, umm... I forgot your name." He had given it to me before and I knew it started with a K.

"It's Kaiser." He held out his hand for me to shake. "And no, I'm not offended that you didn't remember. Even though, I'm memorable as fuck. Mind if I ask where your night went left?"

"Actually, I do." The elevator doors open just in time. I got on and he stood there with a smirk on his face. Giving me a head nod, he bopped off as the doors closed. Entering the apartment, I could smell bustelo on the stove. My mom loved coffee, it was apart of her Dominican culture.

"Hey mami," I spoke in a dry tone while removing my coat and hanging it up on the coat rack by the door.

"Hey baby. How was your day today?" She got up from where she sat at the kitchen table in the living room and kissed my cheek.

"Same as yesterday. Spent all day job hunting."

"Don't you worry, something is going to come through. I can feel it in my bones."

"Ma, I'm so over this. I just want to end it all," I spoke truthfully.

She grabbed my face in her hands and looked me directly in the eye. "Listen to me, god only gives the heaviest battles to the strongest people. You're not going through by mistake. This was destined to happen." I nodded my head in agreement, knowing she'd never steer me wrong. It didn't make me feel less fucked up though. Heading back to my room, I closed the door and turned on my speaker. Music put me into another place and at the moment, I needed to be anywhere but here.

I woke up at seven in the morning in time to submit my claim for unemployment benefits. I hated doing this shit. I felt like I was begging the government to give me money. You would think after the time I put in at my job they would've at least given us a severance package. They didn't give us shit, not even a sorry. Picking up my phone, I dialed the temp agency that my bestfriend Heaven referred me to inquire about any open positions.

"You are in luck Ms. Dozier. There's a receptionist position that just opened down at E Luxe Realty. Are you available to go in for an interview this morning?"

"Yes, yes of course. What time?" I jumped out of bed so quick, my leg got caught in the sheets, causing me to hit the floor. *Fuck,* I cursed, not loud enough for the lady to hear. She read off the address and I was good to go. Unwrapping myself from my sheets, I put up a quick prayer before hopping in the shower and getting dressed. I was going into this interview with it already in my head that I got the job. I had been so down on myself lately, I needed to pick myself up.

The place was in the heart of Manhattan and I knew that finding a parking spot would be near impossible so I decided to take the train. I kept it simple in a a pair of grey slacks, a white silk blouse, and my So Kate heels. I wanted to eat, but didn't want to go through the hassle of brushing my teeth and flossing again, so I opted to grab something once the interview was done.

"Good morning Queen," I said to my mother who was in her bedroom getting dressed for work.

"Hey Princess, where you off to?"

"I have a job interview for a receptionist position at a realty company."

"That's good baby. You already got it." She winked at me and I smiled.

"Thank you ma. I love you. Have a good day and text me once you make it to work." With so many people dying nowadays, it had become a habit for us to text each other once we reached our destinations. You could be here today and gone tomorrow. I for one couldn't imagine life without Kendra Dozier.

Today was going to be a good day, I could feel it. I was able to get out of my building without swatting off a bunch of horny corner boys. There were no delays on the train, so I got to my destination a couple minutes early. Yes, a good day indeed. While on the train, I did some research on the realty company and was shocked to see that it was black owned. Not only that, but they were at competing level with some of the white companies. My heart swelled with pride and I wasn't even apart of the team yet. I loved when my people were in positions to take control and ownership.

Entering the building, I was impressed by the layout. The hues or coral and grey throughout the waiting area was very inviting. Walking over to whom I assumed to be the receptionist, I introduced myself.

"Good morning, my name is Kelly Dozier. I'm here for an interview." My smile was bright and my tone welcoming.

"You must be from the temp agency. Do you have a resume?" Her attitude showed that she wasn't enthused by my presence. I wanted to know when it became customary for a receptionist to ask for an interviewee's resume. Not wanting to be turned away before I even got in for the interview, I swallowed the curse words that were threatening to come out of my mouth. Going into my tote, I pulled out my resume. Just before I could hand it to her, a beautiful man standing at a good six foot three made me pause.

"I'll take it from here. Ms. Dozier, please follow me to my office." He held his hand out to guide me and gave ol' girl a look that said he'd be talking to her soon. I walked ahead like I knew where I was going. I know that bitch was sick throwing up right now.

I stopped short and turned to face him. "I'm sorry, I was such in a rush to get away from her that I'm walking with no destination. I should be following you."

"It's cool, and I'm sorry that your first interaction with Jackie was less than stellar. I'll be addressing that. My office is here." He reached around me and opened the door. "You can have a seat here. Tell me a little bit about yourself and your work background." I gave him a little background and spoke proudly of my work experience. Handing him my resume, the room was silent for a good two minutes and I didn't know what to think. I wanted so bad to big myself up more, but didn't want to do too much.

Not being able to take the silence any longer, I spoke up. "Look, I know that I don't have experience in this field, but I know sales and I love people. Trust me when I tell you that with hands on training I'll be the best receptionist you've ever had the pleasure of working with." I hoped I didn't sound desperate, but I wanted the job.

"Can you be here tomorrow at eight?"

"I can do you one better and be here at 7:45." He smiled and stood with his hand out for me to shake.

"Welcome to the team Ms. Dozier."

"Call me Kelly." I shook his hand and let myself out. I held my composure while walking pass the salty bitch up front. I made sure to wink at her ass as I exited the building. Now, that's how you land a job!

. . .

<u>Tracey</u>

Since Amanda's visit, I had been holed up in the house getting high out of my mind. Her speaking on my motherhood really got to me. She had no right to throw Eniko in my face. I was battling a fucking sickness. Everyone had something to say like I chose to be this way. Addiction is a bitch and right now it had a grip on me so tight that I couldn't see past it. And it wasn't an excuse, just my reality.

Reaching over on my nightstand, I looked in the drawer for my stash and it was empty. "Fuck!" I was out of candy. I had finished a whole eight ball in twenty for hours. Looking over at the clock, it was approaching eleven and I needed something in my system. Stripping out of my clothes, I walked over to my closet to find something quick to throw on. Doubling back, I stared at myself in the mirror and didn't recognize the woman looking back at me. My once healthy 165 pound body now looked like a wasted 140. My mind went back to a time when I was pregnant with Eniko and I'd stand in front of the mirror naked eating butter pecan ice cream while Micah rubbed shea butter all over my body.

"Who you think she gonna look like?" I asked Micah while stuffing a spoon fool of ice cream in my mouth.

He looked up at me with his beautiful hazel eyes and smiled. "I think she's gonna look like me and be smart like you. Ain't that right mama," he spoke to my belly and kissed it.

"I agree. She's gonna be the perfect blend of the both of us. Nothing is better than this moment right here." A tear fell from my eye before I could stop it. I was overwhelmed with extreme happiness. Micah was everything I wanted in a man plus more. He Stood Six Feet Two Inches tall and had a muscular built that most men had to work out daily for. His skin was almond butter smooth and the beard I had convinced him to grow, had the perfect thickness. Sometimes I'd lay in bed next to him and think about what I'd done to deserve him.

"Aww, come on crybaby," he stood to his feet and kissed my lips, "you crying because you happy or because the ice cream almost gone?"

"Both, shut up." I laughed wiping my face.

Absentmindedly, I put my hands on my belly wishing I could go back to that day. I went from sadness to rage, punching the mirror. I couldn't get myself clean enough to get back to that place with my family and that pissed me off. Seeing blood leaking from my hand, I rushed into the bathroom for a first aid kit. I looked like a true crazy person moving about my house naked tracking blood on the floor. Wrapping up my hand as best I could, I cleaned the floor and threw on a sweat suit. This one fitting more snug than before.

Not wanting to run into Kaiser or Micah again, I headed to the Westside of Harlem to find my fix. I didn't care that it was almost midnight and I was lurking in one of the most dangerous tenements in Harlem. The urge I had to get high surpassed all of that. Parking my car, I got out and walked into the park where a group of guys were gathering. I made sure the Nike cap I had on was over my eyes, along with my hoody and my now messed up hand was in my coat pocket.

"Aye, what can I get for $50?" I said loud enough for the group to hear me. They all stared at me like I was an alien from out of space. Now, I know your normal drug users weren't out at this time of night in $200 Milano clothing, but here I was. One of the guys stepped up and I moved back just in case he tried something.

"Take ya hoody off and ya hands out your pockets," he demanded. I gave him a confused look, but complied, not wanting to ruin my chances of getting high.

"Nah man, this her," another guy interrupted, showing something on his phone. "Sorry shorty, we ain't got nothing for you over here." It didn't take long for me to figure out Micah had found away to block my access to my fix.

"Well, fuck y'all," I yelled out pissed. "Y'all ain't nothing but a bunch of runners anyway." Storming off, I cursed Micah in my head. I should've known he would do some shit like this after our last interaction. Pulling my cap back down, I turned the corner and ran smack dead into a woman. "Dammit," I hissed and held my wrapped hand.

"Shit, I'm sorry. Oh, you're bleeding." She held her hand out to me and I waved her off.

"I'm good, I'm good."

"You sure? That hand doesn't look too good." Looking down at the wrapping, I could see blood seeping through it.

"I'ma bout to go take care of it now, thanks." Rushing off, I headed back towards my car. I planned to cruise the streets until I found what I was looking for. I needed something to take the edge off and hopefully numb the throbbing pain in my hand.

"Aye, aye." I heard from behind me, but didn't stop my stride. "Aye, I got what you need." That made me stop and turn around. The guy standing in front of me looked rugged and I was almost positive he got high on his own supply.

"Umm, no thank you."

"Aight, well I guess I'll sell this eight ball to someone else." He faked like he was going to walk away and I the addict in me stopped him. Something in my gut told me not to take the baggy from him, but I felt desperate in the moment.

"How much?"

"The same amount you offered them young boys down the block, $50." He held out the baggy and I gave him the $50 bill. "Nice doing business with you beautiful. The name is D, I'm posted up in building 3150. There's more where that came from." I didn't bother responding, instead I turned and got into my car. Unable to wait until I got home. I fixed myself up right in my car.

It didn't take long before my lip went numb and I started to feel the effects of the high. Only this time, it was different. The way the coke surged through my body made me feel funny. It wasn't the feeling I got when I got high off of Micah's product. I got out the car, thinking I could go after the guy for giving me some bullshit, but didn't make it around my car before I hit the ground.

"Oh my god miss," was all I heard before I blacked out.

Hearing beeping sounds, I slowly opened my eyes and looked down at my arms. Seeing an iv, I instantly shot up in a panic. "What the fuck?!"

"Yeah, what the fuck is right." To my left Amanda sat with a scowl on her face.

"Why the hell am I in a hospital with an iv in my arm?" I asked confused.

"Because your ass overdosed and had it not been for someone seeing you and bringing you hear, yo' black ass would've been dead." Overdosed? I don't overdose. I thought to myself and then it kicked in that the O dude gave me some bad dope.

"Oh my god. The guy from the projects. Oh, I'm gonna go over there and kill his ass. He gave me a bad pack." I was so busy worried about the fact that I had been played that I almost didn't catch the disdain in Amanda's stare.

"Tracey, if you weren't already in that hospital bed, I would sure have done something terrible to put you there. Bitch, you OVER-DOSED and all you can think about is the nigga who sold you the drug. Where they do that at? Where the hell is the nurse because I think you still got some of that shit in yo system forreal." She got up and opened my room door like she was really looking for someone.

"You right, I'm sorry. Mandy, come inside." Hesitantly, she walked back over to me and sat on the edge of the bed. "Thank you for being here for me still. Who was it that you said bought me here?"

"Some lady and thank god she did because your ass was almost outta here."

"Have you spoken to Micah?" I asked, praying that she didn't. I didn't want him to hear about anymore of my fuck ups and this one would've taken the cake.

"Sho' did." I knew her ass was gonna snitch me out. "What? Don't look at me like that? If you're ass had expired he would've been the first to know outside of my aunty and uncle. Seeing as you were close to it, I called him."

"Ughh," I folded my arms across my chest, "what did he say?"

"He didn't say anything other than, hopefully this was your wake up call. He left about an hour ago." Knowing that he was here and didn't stay to make sure that I was okay stung. I mean, I know we we're not on the best of terms, but at the end of the day we're still family.

"Oh, I guess."

"No Tracey, not you guess. This shit should be a wakeup call for you. Do you know I did 80 on the highway when the damn nurse called me? And take me off yo next of kin list because if you gonna be playing with your life I don't want no parts." A knock at the door interrupted our conversation and I was happy it did. "Come in," Amanda called out.

"Hi, Ms. Richardson, I'm Dr. Stevens. I just came by to tell you that you're cleared for discharge. I'm glad that someone was able to get you here when they did. Had the drug went further into your blood stream it would've been fatal. Here are some pamphlets from some programs that I recommend and will help you on your journey to get clean." Removing my iv, she pat my arm, smiled and walked away. I don't know where she got the memo that I was trying to get clean.

"I'll be outside while you get yourself together. Oh, and I had your car towed to your place, so I'll take you home." Getting dressed, I grabbed my purse and my keychain fell out of it. Picking it up, I glared at a picture of Eniko and I when she was about six months old. We had taken a professional photo shoot and my baby looked so peaceful as she slept on my chest. This was a sign. Eniko needed a full time mother and right now I wasn't cutting it. I decided right there that when I walked out of the hospital, I was taking the first step in getting sober. And I needed to do so on my own.

5

MICAH

*W*hen I got a call from Amanda at six in the morning telling me that Tracey had overdosed, I wasn't surprised. I didn't jump out of bed like I normally would. Instead, I laid in bed, staring at the ceiling toying with the idea of going to the hospital or not. I knew I needed to detach myself from Tracey for my own sanity. Still, I got up, threw something on and drove the almost hour drive to Mount Sinai hospital.

Once I saw that she was good and cleared to go home later, there was no reason to sit around. Amanda tried to talk me out of leaving, noting that this was another cry for help. Although I wanted to, I could no longer allow myself to be caught up in my child's mother. She mentioned that it was a woman that found Tracey and brought her to the hospital. I wanted to thank the woman personally and compensate her for being a good Samaritan. Because of her, Tracey would be able to see another day.

Unfortunately, the good Samaritan didn't leave their name or contact information. Before I left, Amanda made sure to let me know that she strongly believed that Tracey was served by someone in the Grant Projects, seeing as that's where her car was towed from. I was fucking livid. I had given specific instructions not to sell to her. If it was one thing I couldn't stand was a person who couldn't follow simple directions. To add insult to injury, whoever the motherfucka was had altered my product.

I'd been in the game for ten plus years and never had anyone od. My shit ain't never been watered down either. I had professional chemist that I recruited, and they made sure my product was 110% at all times. Leaving the hospital, I pulled out my phone and dialed Kaiser. I needed to find the culprit like yesterday.

"Bro, I'm kinda busy at the moment. Let me hit you back," Kaiser answered, his breathing labored. I could hear the distinct sound of moaning in the background. This nigga was fucking and normally I would clown him for it, but right now I wasn't in the mood for jokes.

"Nigga, climb out the pussy. I need every worker from the Grant Houses to report to the House of Horrors in one hour. Anyone there a minute late will be having a up close and personal conversation with my nine."

"I'm on it." He hung up and I got into my car.

I smiled as I drove my car in the direction of the warehouse that I nicknamed the House of Horrors. The name was pretty self explanatory. Some real crazy shit had gone on there and most of it by my hands alone. For those who didn't follow rules and regulations, they were dealt with accordingly. It had been a while since I had to get my hands dirty and I couldn't lie and say I wasn't a little excited. I was a nice guy by nature, but I could also be a sick motherfucka when the situation called for it.

Today was one of those situations. The trip to White Plains was a quiet one. The radio was off as I gathered my thoughts and my mind drifted to a dark place. Pulling onto the street, Karma's jeep swerved into the spot next to me just as I went to park. I knew Kaiser would contact him. Karma's crazy ass never wanted to miss out on a trip to the House.

"I should've known you'd find your way here."

"You damn right. Y'all niggas tryna have all the fun without me." We bumped fist and I chuckled.

"You know I only reach out if I really need you. With your new venture you need to appear as clean cut as possible." Karma had recently opened a club and it's been a hit since the inception of its opening night. Every weekend, he bought the whole city out and made a shitload of money.

"Man, I'm still the same ol' G. Let's go in here and get to the bottom of this shit." He was ready to get shit cracking and he didn't even know why we were here. That was my boy though, he was riding if I was right, wrong, or indifferent. Kaiser, Karma and I had been friends since diapers. Their father was my pops enforcer. Koran was a beast and nothing to be fucked with. He had passed his no non sense approach down to his sons as my pops had done to me.

Walking into the House of Horrors, I surveyed the place to make sure everything was just as I left it. There was an arsenal of weapons hanging along the whole back wall. Throughout the place, there was different torture equipment I used often. Today, I would give the culprit the chance to pick their own method of pain. Eight thirty rolled around quick and I looked on as the workers fouled into the warehouse. Some had signs of weariness, while others looked well rested. One person in particular stood out to me.

I observed everyone as they spoke amongst themselves. Searching for any signs of deceit. D stood off to the side, with his head buried in his phone. Usually, he was talkative and could be heard from the parking lot. Today, it seemed like he had a lot on his mind.

"Ayo, shut the fuck up!" Kaiser's voice echoed throughout the warehouse, silencing the crowd. Walking over to Karma and I, he took his place to the left of me.

Stepping forward, I spoke, "A couple days ago, I gave specific instructions not to sell product to a specific woman. I even went so far as to have a photo sent out to each trap of this woman. Imagine my surprise when I received a call this morning informing me that she od'd on MY FUCKING PRODUCT!" Necks swiveled, as everyone tried to figure out who had went against my wishes. "Somebody better start talking. My shit is the only product pushed in that area."

"Man, I saw D serve that lady after we turned her down in front of building 3150," Ron, one of my lieutenants spoke up.

My gut never steered me wrong. D's eyes got wide and before he could formulate a lie to tell me, I drew on him, hitting him twice in the chest. POW! POW! So much for making him suffer. I was too heated to even get to play how I wanted to. The guys standing closest to him quickly moved to the side just as his body hit the ground. Just as I went to address Ron, another shot went off, but it wasn't from my gun. POW!

"Arghh," Ron groaned, holding his knee. I looked over at Karma who was putting his gun up.

"What?" That nigga said he watched D give T that bad pack. As far as I'm concerned, he's just as guilty as him. Meeting adjourned. Let's go get something to eat." He walked around Ron, toward the exit and I shook my head. Of course Kaiser's goofy ass was laughing and shaking his head. These niggas was nutty.

"Get him to a hospital," I instructed one of the guys from Ron's crew. "Yo," I spoke to Ron, "see Kaiser once they patch you up. Make this the last time you bare witness to someone going against anything that came from up top. Next time you'll find your ass slumped like ya boy D." I waited for everyone to clear out before I called in my clean up guy to get rid of D's body.

Opting out of breakfast with the guys, I headed straight for the office. I wanted to be there when Kelly came in for her first day. After hiring her, I had an extensive background check done. I needed to know who the people I had around me were at all times. So far, she was good. She wasn't running from a crazy past and I didn't need to keep an eye on her. As I drove, my phone rang, my babygirl was calling.

"Hey, little one. You calling to check on me?"

"Hey, dad. Yeah, I had a crazy dream last night and I wanted to call to make sure you were okay." She didn't sound like her chipper self.

"I'm always good Niko. What was the dream about?"

"Umm, I really don't wanna talk about it. I just want you to know that I love you dad. You, Pop Pop, and Aunty Amanda are all I have."

The fact that she didn't mention Tracey as part of her support system hurt me for her.

"Well, it's a good thing I don't plan on going anywhere no time soon. I love you too little one."

"Pop Pop wants to talk to you." I waited for my dad's voice to come through the line.

"What's going on son?"

"Ain't shit, just coming back from handling business. Now, headed into the office."

"How the streets treating you?" Once a month, I put him up on game about how things were moving. Although he had been retired for a while, he still gave his input where he saw fit.

"Everyone's eating." He knew what that was code for.

"Sounds good. And what's going on with Tracey? I sure miss her. It's unfortunate that she got caught up in the life."

I sighed before answering, "Man pops, shit with Tracey is looking even less hopeful than before. This morning I got a called that she overdosed. Thank god someone was there to get her to the hospital. She's so far gone, I don't even think there's no getting her back. And I can't seem to fully shake her."

"Son, I'ma tell you some wise shit that your mama would've said had she been here," he paused and I waited for him to say something meaningful. "If you love something, let it go."

"Man, go head clowning." I laughed and so did he. "I'm thinking you gon' say some shit to make me actually think, so I could make a decision about how I should go about the situation."

"On the real, you gotta detach yourself from her. When she's ready, she'll come around."

"Yeah, she better hope me and Eniko are willing to accept her with open arms." We chopped it up until I got to the office and made plans to link up at his cigar lounge during the week. Entering the building, I found Kelly sitting in the lobby.

"Good morning Jackie. Good morning, Ms.Dozier," I spoke and she stood with a bright smile.

"Good morning, Mr.Hill. I hope you don't mind me coming in a couple minutes early. I wanted to make sure I wasn't late and traffic is vicious on this side of town," she rambled. It was cute.

"Let me show you where you'll be working."

Grabbing her bag, she followed behind me. As we passed Jackie, she grilled Kelly hard. I made a mental note to address it later. I gave Kelly a quick tour of the office, and introduced her to the rest of the team.

"This is your office. As you can see, it's empty with the exception of the desk and computer. We have an interior designer that will stop by later and the two of you can go over ideas of how you want it to look."

"Uhh, that won't be necessary. This is just fine, thank you. This seems like a lot for a receptionist position. Even Jackie doesn't have her own office. I don't want any beef, but I can guarantee that if it's bought to me, I will address it."

"Jackie is my office receptionist. I want you to be my executive assistant. This is my company. When I make a decision, its final. Don't let Jackie bother you. I'll leave you to get situated. If you need anything, my office is across the hall."

Initially, I was going to have Jackie train Kelly, but changed my mind and decided it best that I took on the task. Knowing Jackie, she'd try to sabotage the girl before she could finish her first day. While going over paperwork, I got a text from Amanda.

Mandy: *Hey, they're releasing Tracey today. I'm gonna take her home and make sure she's good.*

I ignored the text and put my phone face down. I knew what Amanda was trying to do and it wasn't going to work. Unless Tracey wanted to talk about our daughter, I didn't have anything to say to her.

Half the day had gone by and I decided to check in on Kelly. Knocking on her office door, I waited for her to answer.

"Come in," she said. I opened the door and found her behind the desk. She had made herself comfortable behind the computer. "You haven't given me a task as of yet, so I decided to do a little reading up on the company." She took the initiative, I liked that.

"I'll have some work for you in a few. Right now, it's lunch time. I'm headed over to the bistro across the street. Join me and I can give you a little more background on the position." She looked skeptical, but got up anyway. At the bistro, we ate and I went over her duties as my assistant. Her job didn't entail much, but her salary would reflect the opposite.

"So, you telling me you're willing to pay me five thousand dollars every two weeks to be your assistant?" She asked with a confused look on her face.

"I am."

"Well, it's your money and if you wanna give it to me, I won't fight you on it."

I chuckled. "Tell me more about yourself. Where you from?"

"Born and raised on the Westside of Harlem. Been here all my life, me and my mother."

"That's wassup. Sometimes I keep late nights at the office. Will that be an issue for your man?" I didn't know where that question came from. I was always out of the office by eight. My ass was just being nosey.

"You just wanna be all up in my business huh?" She laughed lightly. It was a sight to see. "No, there's no man in my life, so I'm good to work late. As far as I'm concerned, the man I had can go to hell."

"Damn, ol' boy must've did a number on you."

"You don't even know the half. I leave the past in the past."

I nodded my head in understanding. I didn't mean to put her on front street, but I needed to know who I was working with at all times. We finished eating and I ordered a chicken salad wrap to go. Kelly was going to be a good fit for the company. Back at the office, we ran into Kaiser in the lobby. The receptionist desk was empty.

"Mann, what you do to Jackie?"

Kaiser laughed. "I ain't do shit to that broad man. She in the bathroom. Wassup beautiful," he spoke to Kelly who smiled and waved.

"I'm gonna head to my office to get started on some of your request. Thank you for lunch. Nice to see you again Kaiser."

"Likewise ma."

Their interaction was real familiar. I watched as she walked away and Kaiser's eyes followed.

"Ay, man keep yo eyes off my employee."

"Shorty bad bro. Not my type though."

"I know, you like em' ratchet." As he went to respond, I spotted Karma coming out of the men's bathroom. Jackie came out a second later with her head down.

"Jackie, we not selling pussy. we selling homes." Her head shot up and she looked embarrassed. Kaiser broke out laughing while Karma shrugged his shoulders.

"I ain't pay her bro, so we good."

"Man, get out my place of business. Whatever y'all came here for we can talk about it at another time." I made sure they left the building before focusing my attention back on Jackie. "This is it for us shorty. You gotta pack ya stuff and get up outta here."

"Micah, I'm sorry. You know me, it's never my intention to disrespect you or your company," she pleaded.

"But, you did, and I can't have a person who makes such poor decisions working here. I gave you an opportunity as promised, but you blew it, learn from this shit and do better. I'm giving you thirty minutes to pack up." It was a good thing Kelly had multi tasking as a skill on her resume; she was going to be doing a lot of it.

6

KELLY

"*These red roses damn near turn to ashes. If I keep it real, you won't understand it. These dirty blogs got your mind damaged. I'll walk a million miles to see you happy..*" I swayed in my chair as Future's verse on Jhene Aiko's, *Happiness Over Everything* played throughout the bookstore/lounge. I had left work over an hour ago and got a call from my bestie Heaven asking to meet up. When she mentioned it was open mic night, I was down.

"I love the atmosphere here," Heaven spoke over the music. While I was still dressed in my pantsuit for work, Heaven was all dolled up. She had on designer from head to toe and I wouldn't expect anything less. My friend was over the top.

"I know. Everyone is in their own world and there's no drama."

"So, how was your first day working with that fine ass Micah Hill?" She licked her lips and leaned forward.

"Umm, first of all, eww. Secondly, it was cool. I'm his executive assistant, so I'll be working closely with him."

"Shittt, I'd be happy to work right up under him."

"You are hot in the twat, you know that right."

"For the right price, I sure am." I laughed as she swayed her hands in the air. The host had gone up to the stage to announce the first poet. "Hmph, they just let anybody up in here don't they." Heaven's face was screwed up like she smelled something foul.

I looked in the direction her head was turned and the woman that walked through the door looked familiar. She had on a revealing dress, but didn't completely fill it out. I hated when Heaven got down on those she felt less fortunate than her. She'd been doing that since we met in High school. Hell, she used to do it to me before we actually became friends.

"Don't do that. We're all one bad decision away from being right where she is."

"The hell I'am. I wouldn't be caught dead outside looking like that."

Seeing the woman head for the bar, something tugged at me and I got up to approach her. Heaven called me from behind, but I kept on walking. Getting closer, her side profile got clearer. It was the same woman I had rushed to the hospital the night before. Seeing her slumped down in front of her car reminded me of the days I had to shake my mother out of that same state. Only there was no shaken this woman. She barely had a pulse when I checked.

My mother was a recovering addict, who had been clean for the last six years. It wasn't easy to see my mother spiral out of control, but I loved her through it all. She fought through her addiction and I commended her. Like my mother, the woman whose name I had yet to get had hit rock bottom.

"Hey, I figured that was you. How are you?" I sat at the bar stool next to her. Her eyes were glazed over and I could tell she was high.

"Oh, hey," she responded while sitting up straight as best she could.

"I don't mean to overstep, but I wanted to come over and ask how everything went at the hospital?"

"Everything went well, thank you. I'm the picture of perfect health." She smirked. I wanted to ask by whose standards, but decided against it. Clearly, she was in denial.

"Well, that's good to hear. I'll be praying for you, umm.."

"Tracey, my name is Tracey. Thank you for making sure I was

good the other night, but I could do without the prayers. You'd just be wasting your breath. God is taking a break from answering any prayers that involve me." She stepped down off the stool and walked away. Seeing that she hadn't began her journey to recovery made me think about the last time I witness my mother strung out. It was the last straw for me and she knew it.

"I can't do this shit no more!" I yelled out as I entered my mother's bathroom where she was laid stretched out with a needle in her arm. I couldn't even cry, sadly, I was used to this shit. Dropping my bag on the floor, I went over to her and carefully removed the needle before throwing it in the sink. Bracing myself, I lifted my mother's dead like weight and put her into the tub. Turning on the water. I knew she was going to curse me out once I turned the shower on, but I didn't give a damn. Twisting the knob, I put the cold water on full blast.

"Wha.. wha.." she tried to speak, but the water drowned her out. Feeling like she had enough as she started to flail her hands, I turned the water off. Taking a seat on the toilet, I grilled her. "What the hell is your problem girl?" She had the nerve to ask me.

"No ma, what's your problem? You not tired of living like this? You were just passed out with a fucking needle stuck in ya arm. Like, come on."

She tried sitting up in the tub, but since it was slippery, she sat back to avoid busting her ass. "Listen here little girl, I'm yo' mama, you not mines. I might be on this shit, but watch ya tongue with me."

Standing up, I snatched up my bag and walked toward the door. "You gonna have to start acting like the mother you wanna be treated like. If you can't then I can't come around no more. I love you ma, but I will not sit around and watch you put yourself into an early grave." I didn't wait around for her to respond.

After that episode, I ignored every call that came from her. It was hard to not be there for my mother like I was used to, but I had to do it for me and her. On the fifth day, I answered the phone. She let me know that she was going to go away for a while and get herself together. I cried because I believed her this time. I didn't hear from her for a month and when I finally got the courage to go over to her house, my mother looked like her old self again.

Gone was the ashy skin, and crusty lips. Her hair wasn't in a raggedy ponytail and best of all, her glow had returned. She was officially clean. I hoped for Tracey's sake that she too would experience that one day.

"Why you over here talking to that lady like you know her?" Heaven stood in front of me with her face still twisted up.

"Stop doing that," I scolded her. Thinking about my mother's own personal struggle made me snappy.

"Doing what?" She played clueless.

"You know what; looking down on people. You are very aware of where my mother came from and it is the same exact place that woman is in."

She sucked her teeth and rolled her eyes. "That's different."

"Oh, yeah? How so?" I folded my arms across my chest and waited for her to answer. When she didn't, I shook my head and walked back over to our table. I didn't come out to argue with Heaven. I had a good day and planned to have a good night.

"Hey, I'm sorry. You know I didn't mean nothing by it," she said, hugging me from behind.

"Yes, you did. I keep telling you that you have to stop judging people based on their outward appearance. You don't know that woman's story. She could have been a millionaire at some point and her life took an unexpected turn."

"I don't know about the whole millionaire thing, but I hear you."

I didn't even reply. My friend would never get it until unfortunate circumstances came knocking on her door. As the night started to wind down, Heaven slithered her way back into my good graces. I'm sure it had a lot to do with the drinks she kept buying me. It was going on midnight and I needed to get home so that I was well rested for work. I knocked back two bottles of water to somewhat flush my system and get home in one piece.

"Kellz, I don't think I'm gonna be able to drive home. I can't even see in front of me without getting dizzy," Heaven slurred. She was drunk off her ass; typical. Throwing her arm around my neck, I braced myself and paced myself as we walked to my car. She would just have to crash at my house because there was no way I was driving out to Jersey to her house. I knew her car was safe because we were both cool with the owner. Once she was situated in the backseat, I got in on the driver's side.

My seatbelt wasn't fasten good enough when my phone went off. Looking at the caller id, it was an incoming call from am unknown number. Usually, I didn't answer unknown numbers because it was either a bill collector running me down or someone that didn't have no business ringing my phone. In my semi drunken state, I broke my own rule.

"Hello," I spoken into the phone as I put my keys in the ignition.

"Hey baby," the voice that belonged to the devils spawn came through my speaker.

"Damien."

"The one and only. Wassup baby." This fool had officially lost whatever mind he had left if he thought I was going to sit on this phone and politic with him.

"Damien, do me a favor."

"What you need baby?"

"For you to GO TO HELL. Twice!" I banged it on him and laughed out loud hysterically, waking Heaven.

"You okay?" She asked with a raised brow.

"Sure am. And you might want to drink one of those water bottles I have back there so you can sober up. I'am not carrying you inside the house." She sucked her teeth, but made sure to crack open that bottle because she knew I was serious.

When I woke up this morning, Heaven was no longer on the couch where she slept the night before. Figuring that she had come down from her drunken stupor and woke up early to head home, I dialed her number to make sure she was good. The phone rang and rang and she eventually picked up.

"You made it home?"

"Not yet girl. Bryson called me early this morning saying he needed to talk to me."

"And what about your car?" I ignored the Bryson conversation altogether. He didn't like me and I couldn't stand his yellow ass.

"I ubered to get it this morning before coming to his place."

"Okay, well I just wanted to make sure you were good. I gotta get ready for work."

"Seriously Kelly? You not gonna ask me what he wanted to talk about?"

"Did he say he was finally gonna leave his wife and stop treating you like a side piece that he hangs up in a shelf until he's ready to play with it?"

"Forget it. I'll call you later."

"That's what I thought. Love you." I hung up the phone and went to get in the shower. Heaven had been in a situationship with Bryson for the last two years and his ass still ain't filed for divorce from his wife. Heaven was so hung up on how "good" he was to her. In my opinion, she was dick silly just like I was over Damien's trifling ass. Me and Bryson didn't get along because I always made it a point to bring up his wife whenever I was in his presence. I wanted his ass to feel uncomfortable.

Again, I rode the train to work today and since I was about thirty minutes ahead of schedule, I stopped at Starbucks. I decided to grab Micah a coffee to thank him for lunch yesterday. While in line, I had an internal battle on whether or not to get him a frappe or a regular coffee with cream and sugar. To me the frappe seemed on the flirty side and the regular coffee was standard business like.

"Good morning, welcome to Starbucks. What can I get for you today?" The barista asked with a smile.

"Hi, I'll take a venti caramel cookie crunch frappe and a grande coffee with cream and sugar." I decided to veer on the side of caution. After paying, I walked the block over to the office taking in the different ethnicities as people walked pass me. Entering the building, I noticed Jackie wasn't at the front desk.

"Good morning, how can I help you?" She was pleasant and welcoming. The exact opposite of Jackie's stank ass.

"Hi, I'm Kelly, Mr. Hill's assistant."

"Oh, it's nice to meet you." She stuck her hand out for me to shake and I motioned to the drinks I was holding. I could've shook her hand, but with all these health scares going on, I didn't know who to trust. I stopped by Micah's office on the way to mines. His door was opened, but he was on the phone. Waving hi, I set the coffee on his desk.

Getting myself situated, I powered on my computer and went to my to do list I set up for the day. As I was getting in the groove of things, there was a knock at the door. I figured it was Micah, so I called out for him to come in.

"Good looking out with the coffee. I didn't have time to stop at Starbucks this morning."

"You good. It was my thank you for lunch yesterday. Sorry about busting in on your conversation."

"It's cool. I was on the phone with my little one." His eyes sparkled when he mentioned having a child.

"Boy or girl?" I leaned forward, resting my hands on my desk, seemingly intrigued that he had a child. Why? I don't know.

"I have a little princess. What about you?" He leaned over on one of the chairs in front of my desk.

"No, no kids for me."

"Damn, you said that like you allergic to them." He chuckled and so did I.

"It's not like that. I actually love children. I just haven't met a guy that I'd want to share that experience with yet."

He nodded his head. "I get it. What about the last dude you were with? What he do to fuck it up?"

I put my hand up to stop him. "Nope, I'am not about to sit here with you and discuss my failed relationship."

Putting his hand up in mock surrender, he smiled. "Aight, I'ma let you have that because I have some phone calls I need you to make. I sent you an email with five candidates for the office receptionist position. As you can see, Jackie is no longer with us. I need you to call those prospects and conduct a phone interview. Pick the one you like best and get back to me by the end of the day."

"What about the girl downstairs? She seems like a good candidate." I hated to be the reason why someone was out of a job.

"She's too touchy feely. Always wants to shake someone's hand when they come through the door. With the way that damn coronavirus is spreading, she got me thinking that she's one of the carriers." I bust out laughing at his serious facial expression.

"You are so wrong for that."

"Shit, you'll thank me later when I don't have to put the building in quarantine. Get to work beautiful."

I blushed when he called me beautiful and walked out of my office. Micah Hill was something else.

7

TRACEY

I watched from my car as Eniko's school let out and children filed out of the building, running to their parents at the pick up line. With a hoodie covering half my head, I searched the crowd for Eniko. I didn't want her to see me in fear of being rejected, so the parking lot was as close as I was gonna get. When the crowd started to disperse a little, I looked on as Eniko walked through it and over to a Cadillac truck that awaited her.

Tears burned my eyes watching my daughter and seeing how much she'd grown. My old driver, Samuel stepped out of the car and held the door open for her to get in. Eniko was beautiful, her long hair was bone straight cascading down her back, a Fendi head band that matched her book bag held it in place. Micah kept our daughter dipped in the finest threads as he had once did me. Taking out my phone, I zoomed in on her and snapped a quick picture before driving off.

Seeing her made it a little easier to make the decision I was about to make, solely on my own. Waking up in that hospital without my daughter and husband even stopping their day for an hour to check on me, just wasn't sitting ok with me. I think at that moment I realize how far I had really driven them away. Even the potency of my drug of choice couldn't help me shake that feeling in the pit of my chest. Someone had once told me, it would take me hitting rock bottom to change. I asked them what the bottom felt like and they told me I would know when I hit it, well now I knew. Driving another twenty minutes, I reached my destination and took a couple deep breaths before stepping out of the car. Getting out, I took a couple steps and stood in front of the Westchester County Rehab Center. I had done some research on the place after running into the same woman who helped me to the hospital. The way she looked at me with empathy and she didn't even know me, did something to me for the first time. Making my way up the steps, I entered the building. It felt like a whole other world. Although the place was bright, you could tell there was little life inside.

"Welcome to Westchester County Rehab, my name is Jozy how can I help you?"

"I'm here to check myself in for inpatient care," I whispered as if someone I knew was going to pop out of a closet and catch me.

"Okay, congratulations in taking the first step to your sobriety and new life." I nodded my head, still skeptical. "I'll get you checked in, I just need to ask a couple questions. Do you have any bags with you?"

"Umm, yes, inside my car I have a suitcase. I only plan on staying for thirty days tho." I let her know up front. I needed the get clean quick remedy.

"Our goal is to get you drug free. Now, while it maybe a quicker process for others, that may not be your case. We'll figure it out along the way." I wasn't feeling what she was saying. It sounded to me like she was saying I'd be there longer. Whatever, we'd cross that bridge when we got there. She went over the program and what I could expect. I felt drained and I hadn't even completed day one.

"Thank you for the information. Is there anyway I could have my own room? I'd much rather go through this process alone."

"Yes, of course. All of our guests have private rooms. We are big on privacy here. I'll have one of the security personnel grab your belongings and bring them inside. How would you like to pay?" I liked how she referred to the addicts as guests.

"Credit card please." I handed her my American Express card and she processed the payment. I needed to successfully complete this program. My relationship with my daughter depended on it. After the payment went through, she escorted me to my room with security following close behind.

My living quarters for the next 30 days was nothing like the Waldorf Astoria. It was the Hilton at best, but it would do. I figured I had to be in an uncomfortable situation before I was comfortable again. The room was equipped with a twin sized bed, a tv, and simple dresser with mirror attached. I also had a phone. As soon as the receptionist was out of my hair, I was taking the bed sheets off and swapping them for a fresh set I bought from home.

"Okay, so you should be fine from here. I'm gonna let staff know that you're checked in and someone will be in shortly to test your urine. Once we get the results, we can get started with the program."

"Wait, is testing my urine necessary?" Although my last high was yesterday, I knew the drugs were still in my system.

"Yes, it's protocol. We have to test new guests to see what's in your system. Remember you're here for help. This is a judgement free zone."

I sighed and shook my head. Everything seemed so intrusive. The two previous programs I'd been in were nothing like this. Fuck it, it had to be done.

"Okay, it is what it is."

"Oh, and lastly, I'm gonna need your cell phone." She held her hand out and I took a step back with my phone tightly in my hand as if she was going to steal it.

"Oh, hell no, my phone? Seriously? How am I supposed to keep in touch with my family?"

"There's a phone here that you can use. Again, it's apart of our policy. If you'd like, I can give you a minute to reach out to your emergency contact on your personal phone."

This was some bullshit and now I was seconds away from walking my ass right back out the same doors I came in through. Hold my phone? What did I look like a fucking seventh grader? Holding my tongue, I sent a voice note to Amanda, letting her know where I was, and that I'd be calling her from the room phone once I got settled. Reluctantly, I handed over my iphone 11 and plopped down on the bed. *Thirty days Tracey, you can do this shit. You're bigger than this.* I coached myself, hoping that it would settle in my mind.

❧

"Arghh, I can't, pleaseee give me something for the pain," I cried out in intense pain as I laid in bed for the third day in a row going through withdrawal. The cramps that shot through my body almost crippled me, making me wish I was dead. I had been crying out for the last twenty minutes and I didn't give a flying fuck how loud I was. "Pleaseee, help me!!" I heard the door unlock and silently thanked god someone had come to my rescue.

"Tracey, you can do this," Grace, one of the staff that was assigned to me coached as she walked over to me. Grace was an older woman, who spoke softly and had been by my side the last few days.

"I can't Grace. Please, can you just get me a little something to take the edge off? This is my first time in a long time withdrawing and it's the worst."

"Now, you know I can't and won't do that Tracey. You're about to complete your third day. I promise, it's gonna get easier by tomorrow."

"I'm tired of hearing that shit," I screamed, but that didn't deter her from stepping closer to me.

"Lord, I humbly come before you on behalf of your daughter Tracey. Lord, you know where this young lady has been and where she's going. The journey may be a long one, then again it maybe short, but I ask that you cover her. Walk her through this break-through she's getting ready to receive. In your name we pray, Amen."

By now, the cramps started to intense, prompting Grace to place her hand on my back. When she did, it felt like she was pulling out all of my anxiety's and some of the pain out of me. My body felt like it was calming down.

"Grace?"

"Yes sweetheart?"

I sniffled as tears rolled down my cheeks. "Thank you."

"Don't thank me Tracey, thank god." She smiled and pat my leg before leaving out. I was far from the religious type, but I did believe in God. Maybe he did get me through this moment.

My room phone rang for the first time since I'd been here. It was Shanice from the front desk, letting me know that today was my first session with the drug counselor. The last thing I wanted to do was sit in front of a counselor after the episode I just had. I told her to give me an hour anyway. I needed to get in the right headspace.

I was still having stomach pains by the time I got out the shower and threw on a pair of jeans and a shirt. This was undoubtedly the worst I've felt since trying to do this twice in the past. Imagine contractions times five and you'll know exactly what I'm experiencing. Gathering myself, I walked down the hall to the counselors office. The overall feel of the rehab center was dark and drab. And that had nothing to do with the décor. It was more so the atmosphere. Standing in front of a door that had the name, Kendra Dozier on it, I took a deep breath and knocked.

"Come in," the woman on the other side said, clearly awaiting my arrival. Twisting the knob, I entered and closed the door behind me. "Hi, I'm Kendra." I watched as she squirted hand sanitizer in her hands and held it out for me to shake. That made me laugh and she smiled. "That ice breaker works all the time. Have a seat."

"Yeah, that was a good one." I giggled and sat on the loveseat in the corner of the office. Her office was colorful and bright. A stark contrast from the rest of the place. It made me feel like I was on an island. For the first time since I'd been here, I didn't feel out of place.

"So, tell me a little about yourself Ms. Hill."

"Tracey is fine."

"Okay, see look, we're getting somewhere already. You're letting me call you by your first name."

"I guess you can say that." I went on to give her a little background on myself, making sure not to divulge too much."

"Well, it seems like you come from a loving family and had a loving spouse. Where did it all go wrong for you?"

"When I started doing drugs," I answered smartly.

"Yeah, I got that part. My question was, where did it all go wrong for you? In other words what events or emotional turns led up to you doing drugs?"

I sat back in the seat and crossed my hands on my lap. Fiddling with my fingers, I thought about lying, but decided against it. It was time to be honest with myself.

"I felt invisible. Although I had my family, Micah, and my daughter, I still felt like I was on the outside looking in. Not that I wasn't happy, but somewhere along the way I lost myself. I honestly thought I had control over my habit, until it started to control me. In my mind, I had the ability to quit when I wanted to. Then, weeks turned into months and months turned into years. Now, I'm here for you to fix me."

"I can only give you tools. It's up to you to fix yourself and from the look in your eyes I can tell that you have a purpose." I bit the inside of my cheek, willing myself not to cry. "How's your relationship with your family today?"

"Everyone is pretty much over me. My parents and I have been estranged for the past six months, and that's solely my fault. My cousin Amanda wants me to win so bad that I find myself pulling away from her at times. I can't even hold a conversation with my ex and my daughter..." I paused to gather myself. Kendra walked from around her desk with a box of tissue and sat in front of me.

"You need to get familiar with that pain and speak to it. Here," she handed me the box of tissues, "let that go."

I let the tears fall freely. "My daughter is getting older and I'm not there to experience life with her. I haven't interacted with her to know what she's thinking, but I know its nothing good."

"Well, our first session is going to be about mending relationships. Over the next two weeks, you'll be reaching out to people you deem most important to you. It's about time you ask for forgiveness, and in turn you'll forgive yourself. Today, I want you to reach out to your daughter."

I shook my head no. "Uh, uh, Kendra no. I'm not ready to do that yet. I'm not even completely sober. Can we do that in the next week or so?"

"Usually, we would, but for you, I believe we should start here." She grabbed a cordless phone from her desk and held it out for me to take. I reached for it hesitantly. "I'll be right here every step of the way. You can do it," she encouraged.

Taking a deep breath, I dialed Eniko's number that I still knew by heart. Once I got to the last number, I hung up the phone. Looking up at Kendra, she didn't appear disappointed, instead she nodded and signaled for me to try again. This time I dialed the last digit to complete the call.

"We're sorry, the number you dialed is no longer in service—." I clicked the end button before the operator could finish crushing my dreams. Distraught, I set the phone down and cried. Kendra walked over and rubbed my back to console me, but I was inconsolable. That failed call just made me realize how far apart me and my daughter were.

I made it through a full week of the program and had been making strides to making amends with my family. I can admit that after the failed call to Niko, I felt defeated, but I pushed through. Yesterday, I called Amanda and apologized for the last two years. I shut her out for a while, but she still managed to come to my rescue whenever I needed her. Today, Kendra wanted me to call my parents. Last night, I thought of everything I wanted to say and what their responses would be. I knew my dad would be open to my apology. My mother on the other hand was a hard nut to crack.

"Alright Tracey, you ready to make the call?"

"As ready as I'll ever be. Can we put the call on speaker? That way you can take over if I get choked up." There was no telling what my mother would say once she heard my voice.

"Sure, no problem." I took a deep breath and dialed the number.

My legs jumped up and down as the phone rang and rang. I went to hang up just as my dad's voice came through the phone.

"Hello," my dad's baritone voice spoke instantly making my eyes water. I willed myself not to let the tears fall.

"Hey dad," I managed to get out. Kendra gave me a thumbs up.

"Tracey, is that you?"

"Yes dad, it's me. How are you?"

"I'm well, my angel. Even better now that I hear your voice. How about yourself?" It made me feel good that he was happy to hear from me. "I'm doing okay daddy. I checked myself into a rehab center and completed my first week today."

"Oh, yeah? I knew you could do it. You just had to make the decision for yourself. I'm so proud of you and I know you gon' kick that program's ass." Kendra giggled and so did I.

"I'm trying to. Is mama around?"

"Yep. She's in the kitchen cooking breakfast for Niko." The mention of my daughters nickname made my heart rate speed up a little.

"Niko's there?" I questioned, in hopes that I could at least hear her voice.

"Not yet. Micah's on his way here with her. When's the last time you two spoke?"

"It's been a while dad," I was ashamed to admit.

"That'll change soon enough. It has to. Let me go get ya mama so the two of you can talk. And just be prepared because you may not like what she has to say, but you know it's coming from a place of love." Instantly, my stomach got queasy. The phone went silent for a moment and then there was some shuffling in the background, followed by some whispering.

"Hello daughter," my mother greeted me. Her tone was one I couldn't detect.

"Hey ma, how you doing?" I figured I'd ask the same questions I asked my father to break the ice.

"I'm blessed and highly favored. Miss seeing your face."

"I miss you too ma. I wanted to call you guys to apologize for cutting you out of my life and disappointing you with my life choices. I know you expect more for me and I let y'all down. For that, I'm sorry and hope that we can get back to where we were as a family. I don't know if daddy told you, but I'm in a rehab program." The phone got quiet and I held my breath hoping that she accepted the apology.

"Tell her we accept the apology," I heard my dad whisper in the background. My dad always had my back even if he didn't agree with my decisions.

"We accept your apology Tracey. All I want is for you to take this time serious. You have lost so much time already, especially with Niko. We never stopped loving you baby, so fight this shit so you can get back to yourself."

"I will and I love you too ma. Let me get back to my session, I'll call you guys in a couple days." As soon as I hung up, Kendra leaned over and hugged me.

"You did so good."

"Whew, that was a lot, but I'm glad I did it. Are we done for the day?" I wanted to get something to eat and lay down.

"Not quite, but I'm let you go early today. Next week you'll make your final call."

"To who?" I silently prayed that she didn't say the call would be to Micah. Preparing to call him was worst than calling my parents.

"Your ex."

"Can I write him a letter? I feel like I can convey my feelings better on paper."

"How about sending an email? If we can do that then we have a deal." She stood and held her hand out for me to shake.

"Deal." We shook on it and I went to walk out when a picture on her desk caught my eye. "Hey, the picture of your desk, the woman looks so familiar." I pointed to the professional picture of a female in a cap and gown.

Kendra smiled while picking the picture up. "That's my angel, my daughter Kelly." Well, I'll be damned. It was the same woman who'd rescued me. I swear God works in mysterious ways.

8

MICAH

"Come on Niko, you look beautiful babygirl," I complimented Eniko as she stood in front of her floor length mirror with her arms folded tightly and her face bald up. She wasn't excited about this mother/ daughter dance at all. I had to practically beg her to get dressed. "Can I at least get a little smile for the picture?"

She gave me a half ass smile and a half of a pose. One of the things Niko and her mother had in common was their attitude. When they had their minds made up that they weren't feeling something, they couldn't be fake about it. I had picked out her outfit myself and my baby was Burberry down. I even went so far as to have her hair dresser come to the house to blow her hair out. The Burberry head-band kept her hair in place while showing off her beautiful round face. That did nothing to change her mind about not wanting to go.

"Daddy, I really, really don't wanna go. Can we just go out to eat or something? I'll even stay dressed up." The doorbell ringing stopped me from answering immediately. I already knew it was Amanda. Hopefully, she could put Niko in a better mood because I was failing big time.

"Hold that thought." Leaving her room, I jogged to the front to open the door.

Amanda entered the house with her hands in the air singing, "Ay, yo where the party at, girls is on the way where the ba.." I held my hand out to stop her before she could finish the lyric.

"Ain't no Bacardi over here, or at the dance. It's a kids party." Her hands dropped and I laughed as she placed them at her sides.

"Well, shit, I need something to get my mind right before I had to be around a whole bunch of pre teens. You know I don't even do kids and that age group is disrespectful as hell. You lucky I love my Niko and will do whatever with in reason to make her happy. Where she at?"

"Right here aunty Mandy." Niko appeared from the back of the house, dragging her feet.

"Uh, uh pretty girl. Why the long face?" You looking too cute to be walking around with that kind of mug." She pulled her in for a hug and kissed the top of her head.

"Daddy making me go to this dance when I told him it was dumb. I'm gonna be the only daughter there with no mother. No offense aunty."

"None taken boo. I'ma need you to turn that frown upside down. We bout to go turn that little school dance out. Look, I even learned how to do the shoo." I cracked up laughing as Mandy broke out in one of the latest dance moves. Niko joined in, laughing too.

"See, y'all gon' be doing all that. I know you don't wanna miss out on it. Not having your mother there doesn't exclude you from anything," I expressed.

"Right. And whoever tells you it does will get they ass beat by me. I don't care how old they are." I looked at Mandy and shook my head. "What? You know these hands do not discriminate and kids are just as bad as adults. Now, get yo jacket and let's go show these people what best dressed really looks like."

Niko smiled big before running off to do as requested. This was one of the many reasons I fucked with Amanda heavy. She would literally drop everything to be there for Niko. I knew she had my daughter's best interest at heart. And best of all, she made sure Niko knew that she could never replace Tracey.

"I'ma drop y'all off and pick y'all up when its over. Here, take this," I handed her an envelope from my jeans pocket. "Thank you again."

She pushed the envelope back to me without opening it. "You already know I don't do this for the money. That's my baby back there. I got her for life."

"I know, but I wanted to give you this as a token of my appreciation. You always go above and beyond for us and I can't thank you enough. It's nothing crazy." I handed her the envelope again and this time she took it.

"Alright nigga, since you forcing it on me, I'ma take it." I chuckled as she slid it into her purse and playfully rolled her eyes.

"I'm ready," Niko announced and we headed out.

❦

After dropping the girls off, I went by Karma's lounge for a drink. It was six now and the party didn't end until nine thirty, so I had time to kill. For it to still be early in the day, the lounge had a nice crowd and the music was rocking. I walked through the crowd and gave the universal head nod to people I knew. I wasn't untouchable, but then again I was. People knew of me, but only a select few were able to actually be in my presence.

"Wassup witcha Micah," Jax, the bouncer saluted me as I approached the entrance to VIP.

"Ain't shit dawg. How you?"

"Another day in the land of the living. I'd say I'm doing good."

"That's all that matters. Them fools up there?" I asked referring to Kaiser and Karma.

"Yeah. They got a couple guests up there too." He winked and I laughed.

"Man, I ain't fucking with y'all. Send Megan up with my usual." Megan was my server. She wanted to fuck ya boy something serious. Unlike Karma, I stuck to the rules and wouldn't fuck his coworkers. I walked through the door and up the steps that led to VIP. The way

Karma had the set up was dope. It was his private VIP section that he had sketched out. With the help of my team he was able to get the room set up like a skybox. Plush couches aligned the walls, along with custom LED tables. The imported tinted glass made it so you could see what was going on on the main floor, but people couldn't see upstairs.

"Oh shit, my nigga done came through to kick it with the common folks. Excuse me mama," Kaiser clowned, moving the half naked female from his lap. I dapped him and Karma who had upped the ante with two females in his lap.

"I'm not here for long. I just dropped Niko and Mandy off to a dance at Niko's school."

"That's wassup. What Mandy fine ass had on?" Kaiser inquired. He still had a crush on her after all these years. Every time he would shoot his shot, she would shoot him down. According to her, she was happy in her relationship. That didn't stop Kaiser from wanting her.

"Umm, excuse me," shorty who was just in his lap said.

"You excused. Don't go acting like we together and shit shorty. I just met you a half hour ago. Put them eyes right back in your head. As a matter fact, I need a break. Take ya girls and clear the room." He shooed the girl away. She was visibly pissed along with her homegirls.

"Damn nigga, that shit ain't have nothing to do with what I had going on," Karma complained. "Them hoes was about to hit me with a quick menage and bobble on each ball."

"Nigga, yo dick gon' fall off. Always wanna get some head," I joked and sat down.

"Betta than this nigga here," he pointed to Kaiser. "My dick go in a lot of bitches mouths, his, another story."

"Aight bro, enough conversation about my piece. That shit sound gay as hell," Kaiser argued. "Pour up my nigga," he invited. On cue, Megan came in with my bottle and a covered plate of wings; my usual.

"Here you go Micah. It's good to see you," she flirted, placing the items in front of me.

"You too shorty. Don't work too hard." I slipped a fifty dollar bill in her shorts and she switched off.

"While she smiling and shit, my dick been down her throat too," Karma said outta nowhere.

"Nigga!" Kaiser and I said at the same time before we all fell out laughing.

For the next two hours, we sat around shooting the shit. My stomach was in knots from laughing at the two of them go back and forth. They couldn't agree on shit other than the fact they loved money, liked to fuck hoes, were both trigger happy, and they would bust their gun for each other. Other than that, Karma and Kaiser were like oil and water. After downing a cup of 1942, I stood up at the glass and watched the people on the lower level.

"Yo, Cah, how things going with Kelly?" Kaiser asked just as I spotted her at the bar arguing with some dude. I didn't answer, seeing the argument start to get heated, I made my way downstairs to intervene.

"Yo, where you going?" Karma called from behind me and I knew Kaiser was right behind him. I made my way through the crowd in time to see dude push Kelly to the ground. I don't know what came over me, but I lost it and hit him in the back of the head with a haymaker. He hit the ground quick. Stepping over him, I went to help Kelly up.

"What the hell?" Some chick yelled pushing through the people who'd gathered around us. "Kelly, are you okay?" She walked over to Kelly who had her face buried in my chest, crying. I was sure it was from embarrassment.

"Back the fuck up and mind y'all business," Karma barked at the patrons who adhered to his request and went back to partying.

"What you wanna do with this nigga Cah?" Kaiser asked while taking a moment to kick dude in the side.

"Damien? Oh my god, what happened to him?" I screwed my face up at the woman who now seemed more concerned with the sleep nigga that assaulted her friend.

"Just get that nigga up outta here before I pop his ass." I looked down at Kelly, "You're coming with me," I said not giving her a choice.

&

"Thank you for helping me out back there. You didn't have to do that," Kelly said while looking out the window as I drove.

"You don't have to thank me for doing what was right. I have a daughter and I would expect the same for her if she were in that same position." I knew for sure that if a nigga act like he wanted to try Eniko Niomi Hill like that, his ass would end up on somebody's obituary. "You know ya friend ain't shit right."

"Who, Heaven?"

"If that's her name, then yeah?"

She chuckled lightly. "A lot of people are put off by her, but we've been best friends for years."

"Shit, if that's how a best friend reacts to you being in distress, I could only imagine a enemy." She turned to me with her face scrunched up like I said something wrong. "Sorry if that makes you feel a way. I had to keep it a stack though. It was like she was concerned with you, then when she noticed dude on the floor, it was fuck you. Who was he anyway?"

"My ex... Damien. The worst mistake I ever made, but figured it out too late."

"Mind if I ask why y'all got into it?"

"He's mad that I don't want anything to do with him; typical shit. After how he did me, he'd be lucky if I spit on his ass if I saw him on fire."

"Oh, that must be the fuck nigga that got you not wanting to have kids. He's a bitch ass nigga for putting his hands on you." I got mad all over again. I hated punk bitches like him. All that energy he had with a woman he'd never give to a man.

"Yep, but it's cool because I'ma fix his ass. I know I can't beat a man, but the next time I see his baldheaded ass sister, I'm on her ass. I never liked her ass anyway."

I laughed at her logic because it actually made sense to me. It was smart. Usually you'd have these women out here tryna buck up at a nigga, only to get knocked on they ass. I was teaching my daughter to never put her hand on a man; shoot his ass.

"I'm gonna see to it that you don't have to do all that."

"That's nice of you, but my mind is already made up. I just want him to leave me alone."

"He will. I'll make sure of it." I pulled the car into the parking lot of Niko's school.

She looked all around before focusing back on me. "What are we doing at a school?"

"Here to pick up my daughter. She had a mother/ daughter dance tonight."

"Oh god, why didn't you drop me off? I'm not in the mood to be getting into it with your woman." She pouted and it was cute as fuck.

"Chill out love, me and my daughter's mother are not together. She's also not here. Eniko is here with her aunt."

"Oh, my bad. Still uncomfortable though, but let me not be ungrateful."

"You good. Here they come." I watched out the window as Amanda and Niko raced to the car.

"Let me get in the back," she went to touch the handle and I stopped her.

"I said you're good. Trust me." I got out to talk to Amanda and Niko before they entered the car.

"How was the dance?"

"Ooh, it was lit daddy," Niko spoke excitedly. "Me and aunty won the dance contest."

"We sho did. I hit my dougie and it was over, right niece." I laughed at how hype Mandy still was.

"I'm glad y'all had a good time. I have my assistant in the car. I'm dropping her home." I directed my attention to Amanda. "She's cool peoples, so be cool."

"Cah, ain't nobody worried about your little assistant. Just get me home, my damn feet starting to hurt." Grabbing Niko's hand, she walked around me and opened the back door. "Hey girl, I'm Mandy. How you doing?" She spoke to Kelly and like the polite little girl I raised, Niko did the same.

"Hi, I'm Kelly. Hey pretty girl," she said to Eniko who smiled. We dropped Amanda off first and then Kelly in Harlem. I knew by the time we got home, Niko would be dead to the world.

"Which building is yours?" I asked Kelly who seemed to be occupied with her own thoughts.

"You can drop me off on the corner. I can walk to my place from here."

"You don't want me to know where you live or something? I can pull up your info on my phone in five seconds ma." I held out my phone for her to see.

"It's not that. You've done enough already and to be honest, I'm still embarrassed about what happened back at Karma's." I stopped the car and looked over at her.

"Kelly, that shit that happened back there you had no control over. We can't erase the past. Shit, we all got some shit going on in our lives. Yours just happened to be put on front street tonight. I know I'm perfect, but I got some life shit going on too." I thought about Tracey and shook my head.

"Perfect? Boy bye." She laughed and I smiled.

"See, smile. Life's good ma. Now where's your building?" She pointed to the middle of the block and I drove in that direction.

"I'm right there," she pointed to a building in the middle of the block. She lived directly across from Grant Houses. Now I was wondering if she didn't want me to drop her in front because of that.

"Ay," I called out from the window once she got out, "make sure you text me when you're in the house, so that I know you made it in safe."

"Will do." I waited until she was inside the building before pulling off.

"Daddy," a sleepy Niko called out to me.

"Yes princess?"

"I like her. Y'all should hang out more." Great minds thought alike, because I was thinking the same thing.

§.

Over the next couple days, I found myself spending more time with Kelly. She was cool to hang out with. I came to find out that we liked most of the same things. Outside of work, she liked to eat, read, and chill. That's what our time together usually consisted of. I would find ways that made sense for us to have lunch together while at work.

During those times, I made sure we tried different foods, even if that meant ordering in and eating in my office. She was easy to talk to and made it her business to not let the friendship that seemed to be budding between us get between her work. We hung out so much, I found myself thinking about her when I wasn't at work. I thought it strange that my new assistant had found a way to preoccupy my thoughts even when I wasn't in her presence. Not wanting to admit what was really going on, I went to check in with my dad to make sense of it all.

"If you here without Miss Lady then you must be in trouble."

"I wouldn't say that I was in trouble. In need of advice sounds more like it." I gave him a manly hug and stepped inside of his office where he stayed holed up for hours. I remember him doing the same thing when I was a kid.

"What's going on son?"

"Pop, I'm feeling my assistant. And not just on no sexual shit either. We got a real good vibe going on. I like being in her company."

He sat back in his chair and peered at me. "It's been a while since I've heard you say you enjoyed a woman's company. I think the last time I heard that, you bought Tracey around."

"Yeah, this is a different vibe though. I can't put my finger on it, I just know its different."

"Then let the vibe do its thing. If you keep thinking too much about it, it's a sure way to fuck it up." I looked at him and smirked. In under two minutes he had the answer to my troubles.

"How you still manage to do that shit after all these years?"

He chuckled. "It's a gift. That's why I'm the father and you're the son." He was right, I needed to let things play out. Besides, the get to know you phase was where you figured out who a person really was.

9

KELLY

oday was my one month anniversary at E Luxe Realty. I thought for sure that I would quit after Micah had to practically rescue me at Karma's lounge. I contemplated not coming into work on my next scheduled day, but I was far from a quitter. I walked in that Monday with my head held high and Micah interacted with me as if the incident never happened.

I had successfully managed to complete the task of hiring a skilled office receptionist. Not only did she work out well for Micah, but for the office as a whole. As executive assistant, I'd taken on all things Micah. Making it easy for he and I to develop a close business relationship. He trusted me to make decisions when it came to the business and had even set me up to take some real estate courses online to get my license.

I loved the role I played at the company. An even bigger perk was the pay. It afforded me the ability to secure my own apartment in a high rise, not too far from the office. I slipped up one day and mentioned my living arrangement with my mother to Micah, during one of our business luncheons. I wasn't complaining, more so stating that soon I'd have enough saved to move. When I returned back to my office that day, there was an email in my inbox with information about an available unit in a luxury apartment building. I quickly jumped on it after seeing the price for rent.

That evening when I showed up to see the place, Micah was there handing over the keys to my new place. I was happy as hell, but a little apprehensive at the same time. I didn't take handouts and it wasn't because of my pride either. I believed in working for what you want and being able to brag that you paid for it. So, although he offered the place to me as a company gift, I refused and had been placing a check on his desk every first of the month to cover rent. Kelly Dozier was the epitome of an independent woman.

This morning, I prepared notes for the monthly team meeting. It took no time for the agents to get used to me being around. We'd developed a cool relationship, especially Domonique and I. That was my girl. She kept me laughing and was always available for any questions I had about my online courses. Entering the boardroom, everyone was seated and greeted me as I sat next to Micah. Dominique was set to present and we all gave her our attention.

While she spoke, I discreetly looked over at Micah and took notice of how distant he was. It was clear that he had a lot on his mind as he alternated from Domonique's presentation and looking at his phone. Unable to focus myself, I took it upon myself to dismiss the meeting, hoping I wasn't overstepping.

"Hey, D I'm sorry to interrupt, but can we pause for a few? I need to talk to Micah for a minute." All eyes went from me to him.

"Clear the room and we'll re convene in a few," he said backing me. Everyone nodded and did as he asked. "Wassup? Everything alright?" He questioned as if he wasn't the one preoccupied.

"I was gonna ask you the same thing. You look like you got a lot on your mind."

"I'm straight. I got a text from my sister Macey letting me know that she's coming in from Miami and wants to go out to dinner with me and Eniko's mom."

"Oh," was the only thing I could come up with. I felt a twinge of something in my chest. It felt a lot like jealousy. Disregarding it, I asked another question. "What's the deal between the two of you? If I'm overstepping, please tell me."

"You're not. Trust me, I would've let you know. Tracey and I haven't been together in a minute. She struggles with addiction and is hell bent on fighting her family and I tooth and nail about getting her clean. Macey knows this, but feels like there's still hope for us once she comes out on the other side of the addiction."

"What do you think?" I let slip. Internally I curse myself, hoping I didn't show my hand.

"Honestly, I thought the same up until last month when I gave her the option to choose between drugs and our family. When she chose the high, that was it for me."

"Wait, what did you say her name was again?" My mind went into overdrive.

"Tracey, why wassup?" My hand went up to my mouth as the name sink into my memory. Tracey, his child's mother was the same woman I'd encountered on different unfortunate occasions. I admitted how I knew her and the time we'd been in each other's presence.

"Wow, this is crazy. Had I known I would've mentioned it way before."

"You really are an angel you know that." He took my hand in his and squeezed it. "Thank you for reacting with your heart and not leaving her for dead. You're a dope ass person. It's a good thing ol' boy fucked up." I didn't know how to interpret that last comment, but it made me smile inside. Caught up in the moment, I leaned in and kissed his lips. When I felt my lips being spread by his tongue, I jumped back like his mouth was on fire.

"Shit," I whispered while touching my lips, "I'm sorry." I raced out of the office before he could respond.

For the remainder of the day, I locked myself in the office. I avoided Micah at all costs. Staying on top of my job, I sent all communication via email. I couldn't bare looking in his face after I played myself. Although he seemed into the kiss I had definitely crossed a line that I so desperately tried not to even teeter on. *Bitch, I can't believe you did that. How you gon' go put ya lips on that man, uninvited at that.* I scolded myself as I typed up my itinerary for the next day and went over payroll.

Today was the first day I acted on the feelings that I was developing for Micah. Being around him day and day out I found myself more and more intrigued by him. He was all business at the office, but when it was just he and I, he was just Micah. The feeling of his lips against mines was everything that I imagined and more. My ringing cell caught my attention and it was a good thing it did. Picking it up, I was surprised to see Heaven's name on my screen. We hadn't spoken much in the past month.

I tried to act as if what Micah said about Heaven's lack of concern for me didn't bother me, but it did. It was easy to dismiss her shady ways when no one was there to point them out. Micah had hit the nail on the head. Her concern for Damien made me look at her through questioning eyes. I thought back to the times she would try to get me to talk to him after our break up despite my obvious disdain for him. I would hate to think that she was the reason he knew where we were that night.

After letting the phone ring a few times, I answered, "Hello."

"Damn Kellz, I was wondering if you were gonna answer. What you up to?"

"My bad, I'm getting some work done. It's been a busy day," I lied.

"Oh, okay. Well, I miss you. We haven't spoken much in the last few weeks, so I wanted to check in."

"Miss you too," I lied again. I loved Heaven, but her actions as we got older had me reevaluating the role I wanted her to play in my life. "I've been really caught up in work lately."

"I get it. Bryson said that its been a while since you've been in the work field, so you may be busy."

"Wait, what? Why is Bryson even discussing me? And how does he know how long I have or have not been employed? You telling my business to ya fuck buddy now?" Now, I had an attitude.

"It's not even that serious Kelly, and he's not my fuck buddy. He was just giving me advice since I hadn't spoken to you. You act like I told him something personal or something." Her dismissive comment pissed me off even more.

"It is that serious Heaven. I shouldn't even be a topic of discussion between the two of you. And the fact that you think it's okay has me questioning you as a friend." I told her straight up. My annoyance wasn't just coming from this current issue, but I was thinking about the other issues we'd had that I buried.

"Okay, you're right, I'm sorry." She used the same five words every time she acted like she was taken responsibility for her bullshit. "We cool?"

"Yeah, we cool," I said not even believing myself.

"You never told me what happened that night at Karma's with Damien. All I know is, one minute I left you standing at the bar to go to the bathroom, then I come back and all hell has broke loose."

"There's not much to tell. Damien put his hands on me because I didn't want to talk and in turn, someone put their hands on him. The end." I smiled thinking about Micah defending my honor.

"That's crazy. I seen him a couple days ago too. He was asking about you."

"Okay."

"He told me he wanted to apologize about what went down, so I kinda told him where you worked. I didn't tell him what days though." She quickly tried to recover.

"You what?!" I yelled into the phone. "Why the hell would you do something stupid like that? He pushed me on the ground, in a crowded club Heaven. I don't know what he's capable of doing."

"Come on Kellz, do you think I would've given him that information if I thought he was a danger to you?" Oh my fucking god, this girl was simple simon forreal.

"After today, I don't trust your judgement at all Heaven. Let me get off this phone before I say something I won't regret." I hung up the phone and threw it on my desk. Heaven's head was so far in the skies that it was ridiculous. I continued working well on the computer well into the evening. A message from Domonique popped up on my screen asking if I was busy. Responding no, she let me know she'd be over in a minute. Stretching out, I sent a text to Micah letting him know I'd be leaving the office soon. He responded, to let him know before I left the building.

"Knock, knock," Dominique said while peeking inside my office. "Hey, boo."

"Hey darling, come on in." She walked in and sat down. "How'd the presentation go?"

"You know I did the damn thing baby. You already know this." She held her hand out and we slapped fives. "How's things with yo boo?"

"My boo?" I asked confused.

"Yes girl. Yo boo, the boss man."

"Get out my office Domonique," I laughed signaling with my hand for her to leave. "Don't go starting no rumors."

"No need to. Y'all chemistry speaks for itself boo."

"Whateva. I don't know what you talking about. How'd your showing go in Long Island?" We talked some more and by the time eight o' clock rolled around the building had cleared out with the exception of Micah and I. As requested, I texted Micah to let him know I was leaving. He wanted me to wait for him to walk me to my car, but I opted out of it. I still wasn't ready to face him. The parking lot was quiet, making me put some pep in my step to get to my car.

"You shouldn't be out here alone." The voice from behind me, made me stop suddenly. I placed the voice on the first word he spoke. It was Damien.

"Damien, I'm letting you know right now, if you put your hands on me, I'm gonna light your ass up with this pepper spray." As I spoke, I reached into my purse to grab the pepper spray that resembled lipstick. Turning around, I held it in my hand with my finger on the nozzle. He held his hands up in the air with a smirk on his face. I still couldn't understand how someone so handsome could be so soulless.

"Aye, I come in peace. I wanted to apologize about what happened back at the lounge. I shouldn't have put my hands on you." He stepped closer to me and I held the pepper spray up.

"Back up. If you step any closer, I will burn your fucking eyes out." Quicker than I expected he grabbed me up by my shirt, making the pepper spray fall to the ground.

"Let me go," I spoke through gritted teeth. I was scared, but I didn't want him to know that.

"Oh, I can't touch you now? You got some new nigga sniffing yo pussy now?" He was so close to my face, I could smell the winter fresh on his breath.

My eyes got wide when I saw Micah approach with his hands on his lips and a gun in his hands. I didn't nod my head or anything, I just stared directly at him.

"You got five seconds to unhand her before I make it so that you have a closed casket funeral," Micah's voice was menacing as he spoke. "One..two..fi—" As soon as Damien let me go, Micah slammed him to the ground and began to pistol whip him. I froze, not knowing whether or not to stop him. The thought of him going to jail and loosing everything, including his daughter entered my mind. Quickly snapping into action, I reached down to pull him off of Damien.

"Micah, come on, that's enough." My pleas fell on death ears. "Think about Eniko!" I yelled out and he stopped mid swing. He stood, and turned to me, and I was mortified. His shirt had splattered blood on it as well as his hand. Not saying another word, I pulled him in the direction of my car. Securing him in the passenger seat, I took another look at Damien who I could tell was still breathing by his chest moving up and down slowly. Shaking my head, I got in my car and pulled off in the direction of my house.

"Go to my house," Micah finally spoke and reclined his seat back, putting his hand over his head. Noting that I wasn't in the position to ask any questions, I did as he asked and went in the direction of his house.

My hands shook as I drove. I was scared to death that Damien would die and I would be responsible. Of course I hated him, but I didn't want him to die. I looked over at Micah who was eerily quiet, typing away in his phone. I was confused as to how he could be so calm after what he'd just done. Even worst was that it didn't make me want to run from him. In fact, I wanted to be closer. We pulled up to his house and using his clean hand he entered the code into the gate.

"Look, that person back there is not someone I want you to get familiar with. That Micah isn't for you. I don't want you to loose any sleep over what happened with ol' boy. I got that taken care of. Do you trust me?"

Without a thought I answered, "Yes."

"Alright, I need to make a run. Niko is with my dad for the weekend. Go inside and get comfortable. There's a guest bedroom near mines. You've been here before, so you should be familiar. I'll take you home in the morning, when I know things are good."

I nodded my head yes and didn't protest. Instead, I reached over and kissed his succulent lips for the second time tonight. This time, I didn't jump back when his tongue parted my lips. After an intense make out session, I got out and used his spare key to enter the house. Looking back, I watched as he got out and entered through his garage. I knew there was a spare bathroom there where he could change. I didn't know what the outcome of tonight would be, but I did know as long as Micah was in my corner, I'd be good.

10

TRACEY

"Okay boo, you ready?" Amanda asked as she put the final touches on my hair. I'd finally reached the 30 day mark at the rehab center, and today was my graduation. It had been such a trying time facing my demons and accepting my truths with Kendra. That woman was truly a god send. I went through countless night sweats during my withdrawal, and on a few occasions she stayed up with me on the phone late nights to coach me through them.

Not only could I credit my getting this far to Kendra, but to Grace as well. She held me down and often fixed me right up when I threatened to quit the program. She would remind me of who and what I was doing it for. Eniko's face flashing in my head put everything into perspective.

"I'm so damn nervous Mandy." I stood up and started to pace the floor. My palms got sweaty and I started to feel anxious.

"If you don't stop that damn pacing. You making my damn head hurt. Why you nervous?"

I stopped pacing and looked right at her. "This shit is really happening. Like, I checked myself into this rehab, by myself. With through the motions, and completed this shit by myself. I actually stuck to it and to be honest with you, I wanted to quit everyday."

She walked over and wrapped her arms around me. "And this is your moment, so cease it boo. It's been a long time coming and while I knew you could do it, I also knew you had to do it for yourself. We need to be celebrating not doing this crying shit." She wiped her own tears that started to fall as well as mines. "Okay, come on, let's do this."

I took another look in the mirror, pleased with my progress. The Emilio Pucci dress Amanda bought for me to wear fit me perfectly. I wasn't as thick as I'd been before the drugs, but I knew with the proper diet, I'd be there in no time. And when I say proper diet, I mean stuffing my damn face with everything but red meat. Amanda walked ahead of me while I peeked into the auditorium to see if I saw any familiar faces.

"Did you tell everybody about today?" I questioned when I couldn't spot any of my people.

"Yes girl. Now, get off my back and go get ready to do the damn thing." She threw up some kind of sign, before walking inside to find a seat. I took a deep breath and followed. I was set to sit on the left side of the room with the other graduates. When I got to the second row, on the right I could see my parents holding hands. Like a child reuniting with their family after a summer at fresh air fund, I fell into their arms. Tears fell down my face freely and I was happy that I opted out of wearing makeup.

"Thank you so much," I said to the both of them.

"No need to thank us. You did this on your own," my mother replied, "I'am so very proud of you Tracey." She wiped my face and my dad kissed my cheek.

"Go on up there and get that certificate my angel." I hugged them again before heading to my seat. My eyes surveyed the place once more, searching for Micah and Eniko. When I didn't spot either of them, I sat down. I was disappointed and even hurt, but I couldn't let it consume me. Not at the moment at least.

"Tracey Richardson," Kendra called my name. Both my parents and Mandy jumped up screaming my name, making everyone laugh. I walked up to the makeshift stage and accepted my certificate. I couldn't have been more proud of myself for sticking through it and taking the program one day at a time.

Once everyone picked up their certificates, we all made our way to the cafeteria to eat cake. To have my mom and dad laughing, talking, and being overall happy in my presence made my heart swell. It would have made the moment that much sweeter if Eniko and Micah were there to share it with me. As I looked around, I watched as kids embraced their parents and thought about my baby. I needed to see Niko's face to make this thing worth while.

"Congratulations," Kendra shouted with her arms outstretched for a hug.

""Thank you so much. I couldn't have done it without your guidance. I appreciate you more than you know Kendra."

"Remember, I only gave you the tools. You did everything else. I commend you for taking on every task I gave you, even the times when you fought me on it." I laughed thinking about the hell I gave her about emailing Micah. She put my hand in hers and smiled. "You take care of yourself and beware of your surroundings. Anything can trigger you and the last thing you wanna do is be back here. Trust yourself enough to be strong." She went to walk away and I stopped her.

"How'd you get so good at this?"

"I once needing saving myself." She winked and moved through the crowd. I had my suspicions that Kendra may have been an addict in the past and she just confirmed it.

"Hey, daddy and I made reservations at one of the steakhouses a couple blocks from here. Don't worry, they have seafood as well. Come on so I can put some more meat on these bones of yours." My mother joked about my weight, knowing she was dead serious. It had been so long since I ate at an actual restaurant. My mouth watered at the thought of a miso glazed salmon. If the restaurant we were going to didn't have it, they'd better be prepared to have it specially made for me.

❦

Eating and laughing with my parents after six months was so refresh-
ing. We didn't talk about the past and what led up to this point. We
just thoroughly enjoyed one another's company. My mom bought up
Eniko and how she was glad that I was going to get a chance to
reunite with her.

"Have either of you spoken to Micah about coming to support me
today?" I asked while eating.

"I spoke to him," Amanda answered.

"And you told him about today?"

She picked up her drink and took a sip before answering noncha-
lantly, "I did."

Now she was pissing me off. "And what was his response?"

"He told me to tell you congratulations."

"That's it? That's all I get is a dry ass congratulations? He didn't
even have the decency to bring my child to see me. Unbelievable." I
put my fork down, pissed.

"Your language Tracey," my father checked me.

"I'm sorry daddy, but this is wrong and y'all know it." I glanced
over at my mother to see if she would jump in at any time. "Ma, do
you think I'm wrong?"

She paused to address me. "I don't think you're wrong for wanting
to see your child. I also don't think he's wrong for not wanting to
bring her. The two of you need to sit down and have a conversation
about what's best for Eniko."

"Wow. You don't think he's wrong for not wanting her to witness
this milestone? Do you know what it was like being in that place for
thirty days and having to fight that demon called addiction?" My
voice raised and cracked as I got emotional.

"No, I don't know because I've never had to do that. Let us not
forget that you are the reason you had to do that. So while I'am over-
joyed that you came out on the other side of your addiction, don't
think that everyone is going to be as welcoming. Just like you had to
make the decision to get clean, people have the right to choose when
they are ready to accept you back into their lives."

"I won't keep apologizing for being an addict. All I can say is I'm better now and I have the right to be able to access my child. If it's okay with you, I'd like to take my food to go." I stood and grabbed my purse from the table. Giving my dad a kiss on the cheek, I did the same with my mother. I walked out of the restaurant forgetting that I didn't drive my car.

"Tracey, wait," Amanda called out to me. "Here, I got your food. Where you tryna go with no car girl?"

"I need you to take me to see Niko."

"Okay, let me hit Micah up to let him know we're coming by."

"I don't need permission to go and see my child Amanda," I snapped at her. "I'll text him myself." Pulling out my phone, I sent Micah at text message.

Me: I want to see my daughter.

There was no need to tell him that I was on my way over. I wanted to catch him off guard. Eniko was my child too, and I had just as much rights as him. I know Amanda was probably pissed at how I came for her, but that was the least of my concerns. All I knew was I wanted to lay eyes on my child and nobody was going to stop me.

When we pulled up to the gate, I started to get anxious. Butterflies formed in my stomach. This was the house that made me a woman. The same house that I birthed Eniko in. I remembered the day like it was yesterday. I pushed out a seven pound, eight ounce baby girl in a birthing pool inside of my living room. All under Micah's encouragement and a midwife's coaching. Shaking my head free of all the happy memories, I mentally prepared for a fight.

"Mandy, whose that woman that just got out of Micah's car?" I stuck my head out the window, damn near breaking my neck to see up the long driveway.

"Ooh girl, I don't know. Give me a second, let me zoom in with my super vision. Bitch, I can't see from here!" She waved me off before reaching over, entering the code to open the gate. Pulling her car into the driveway, as soon as she parked, I went to step out and she pulled me back by my arm. "When you knock on that door, I don't care what you see on the other side of it. Unless Eniko is in danger, you better not go in here and start no clowning."

I snatched my arm back from her. "I don't need you to tell me how to act." Getting out, I jogged up the few steps and rang the doorbell. I couldn't make any promises to her about what my reaction would be if I saw anything crazy. When my door opened, anything I may have had to say got caught in my throat the moment I saw Eniko on the other side of it. The perfect blend of Micah and I. Her hair was pulled back in a ponytail and she had on a gap sweat shirt with matching leggings.

"Hi," she spoke dryly.

"Hey, angel," I replied back nervously, calling her by the nickname my dad gave me when I was younger. I reached out to touch her and she jumped back like she was afraid of me. I felt like shit. I went to say something about it and Mandy's voice could be heard from behind me.

"What's the tea niece?" Mandy greeted and Eniko's face lit up and she side stepped me to get to her. I couldn't even be mad at her. I was mad at myself, but Micah would share in this blame.

"Everything good?" I heard Micah's voice before I could see his face. When he rounded the corner and saw me, his facial expression showed shock.

"Surprise to see me?" I questioned. "We need to talk."

11

MICAH

I didn't know what to make of Tracey standing at my front door. What was even more confusing was her standing here with an attitude. My eyes shifted to Eniko who was practically hiding behind Amanda then back at Tracey.

"Come here Niko." She did as I asked and I pulled her behind me.

"What you doing all that for? You think I'm a threat to my child or something?"

"Right now, I don't know. I do know that if you don't pipe the fuck down with all that hostility, we gon' have to do this little reunion another day." I didn't want to raise my voice with Niko standing here and Kelly in the kitchen. Deciding that we'd been congregating at the door for too long, I stepped back so that she and Amanda could enter. Tracey walked in first and didn't wait for any direction. She walked toward the living room like she still lived here.

"I tried to give you a heads up but she stopped me," Amanda finally spoke once Tracey was out of earshot.

"What is she here for?"

"She graduated the program today, remember?"

"Again, why is she here?"

"Come on Micah, she wanted to see Niko. I figured you wouldn't come to the graduation, but you could've at least gave me a heads up."

Not that I had to explain anything to her, I did anyway. "Look, I'm happy for her, but that wasn't the setting for a meet up. At least I didn't think so."

"Understood. Let's go figure this shit out." I followed behind her, into the living room where Tracey and Niko sat opposite of each other. The both of them looked awkward.

"Hey Micah, I'm gonna head out. Thank you for letting me use your car," Kelly said while walking from the kitchen. It was clear that she was clueless to the foggy air she'd just walked into.

"What the hell are you doing here?" Tracey shouted out, getting up to approach Kelly.

"Yo, you deadass right now?" I intervened while blocking her path. "Niko, go to ya room so I can talk to your mom real quick." She nodded her head and did as I asked with Amanda following behind her.

"See you later Ms.Kelly," Niko said, further adding insult to injury.

"Really? You had this bitch around my child Micah? That's how you get down now?" I stepped back to get a good look at her. I needed to know exactly where this spicy energy was coming from.

"Okay, I understand that seeing me may be a shock. Trust me, I feel the same way. What I'm not gonna do is sit here and allow you to call me out my name," Kelly countered.

"Bitch please. You can save that whole speech for when your walking out the door."

"Yo, chill the fuck out. You," I pointed at Tracey, "no longer reserve the right to question who I have in my home or around Niko."

"See, that's where you're wrong. Anything or anyone that's around that little girl back there, I reserve the right to question."

"Oh, I get it. You've been sober a full thirty days and now you run shit huh?" Her facial expression went from tough to embarrassed. I knew what I said was a low blow, but she was pissing me off.

"I'm just gonna go. I'll Uber home Micah. Again, thank you." Kelly tried to walk off, but I stopped her.

"You ain't gotta do that. I'll call Kaiser to come and take you to your car." The car that she refused to upgrade had died on her last week and I let her borrow mines after putting her own to my mechanic. Today, she was dropping my car off to pic up hers.

"No, its cool. I already ordered the Uber. He should be right outside the gate."

"Exactly. Let her go about her business because you have your own to tend to right here," Tracey added, still grilling Kelly.

"Micah, if you don't let me go right now, you're gonna have to pick your baby mother up off the floor. I'll call you later." I hugged her and whispered in her ear that that gangsta shit was a turn on. After letting her out, Tracey was on my ass like white on rice.

"Why was she here Micah?"

"You know, you sure got a lot of animosity toward someone who saved ya life."

"She told you that huh? Boy, bitches be so desperate for the dick and a couple dollars."

"Trust me, she works for every dollar she gets. And who said we were fucking?" Kelly and I hadn't even taken it there yet. I wouldn't consider what she and I were doing dating. We both enjoyed each others company. I went into the kitchen to get a bottled water and of course Tracey was on my heels.

"You don't have to lie Micah. She seemed familiar with the place, so I'm sure she's been here on more than one occasion."

"Why are you hear Tracey?" I asked, wanting her to get to the point.

"I'm here because I want to be apart of my daughters life. I'm clean now and in a better headspace. I'd like to be able to be around my child without you being involved."

"You see, I was with you until you mentioned me not being involved. I know you're trying to find your way, but there's no such thing as me not being involved."

"I don't need you to teach me how to be a parent."

"Really? Well let me spit some real shit to you. You made the decision to not be a parent. You had many opportunities to come and fix the relationship with our daughter. That little girl has cried on my shoulder many a nights because she thinks you don't love her. So, excuse me if I question your parenting skills." She had me fucked up if she thought her popping back up was gonna be a dictatorship.

"I was sick! How long y'all gon' hold that shit over my head? Would you have rather I stayed and acted like everything was okay and got high in front of her instead?"

"No! I expected you to be a fucking mother and to choose your child over your high!" I barked back with the same energy.

"Alright, back to your corners," Amanda intervened. There's a fragile child in the next room whose life has just been turned upside down. Now, is not the time to place blame and discuss what could've or should've happened. The main focus should be Eniko. Y'all can deal with y'all shit at another time."

Amanda was right. I was so pissed at the way Tracey was coming at me, I had forgot about the innocent person in this whole situation. Both Tracey and I needed to put our issues aside to focus on Niko. Heading towards her bedroom, I stopped and knocked on the door.

"Niko, it's dad. Can I come in?"

"Just you daddy," she said, making it clear that she didn't want Tracey around. I could see the defeat and sadness in Tracey's eyes.

"Give me a minute to talk to her." I opened the door and closed it behind me. Niko lay across the foot of her bed with her beats headphones over her ears, staring at the ceiling. I laid down next to her in the same position. "What's on your mind kid?"

"Is she really clean this time?"

"She says she is. Aunty Mandy said she completed her drug program today."

"Well, what do you think?"

I didn't know what to think. Tracey did look better than she did when I saw her last. "I can only tell you what I know Niko, and that's that she completed her thirty day program today and appears to be sober."

"How am I supposed to feel though? I can tell by her reaction at the door that she wanted me to welcome her with open arms. I just don't feel that way at the moment. Does that make me a bad person?"

"No Niko. It makes you human. If you're not ready to be welcoming, that's okay as long as you're respectful. She made some bad choices, but at the end of the day she's still your mother." I didn't want her faking like she wanted to be around Tracey, but respect would always be due.

"I can do that. How do you feel about her being back?" She turned to face me and awaited my answer.

"I don't feel anything. My goal is and will continue to be to do whats in the best interest of you. I have nothing for your mother other than my partnership in co-parenting you."

"I hope not because Ms.Kelly would be real mad." She smirked and I laughed. I already knew what she was getting at and I wasn't going there with my eleven year old.

"You wanna go hang out with ya aunt and mom for a few hours?"

"C'mon dad, it's too soon. I'm not tryna be out here faking the funk."

"Aight, I get it. I gotta head out to work in a few so I'm gonna drop you to Pop Pops."

"Okay, cool with me."

"Come say bye to your mother real quick. And I know you remember that she likes to hug a lot, so let her hug you and hug her back." We got up together and I opened the door. Back in the living room, Amanda and Tracey were engrossed in a conversation.

"Are you okay?" Tracey asked Niko.

"Yeah, I'm good." There was an awkward silence before Niko spoke again. "Congratulations on completing your program."

"Thank you. I appreciate that. Look Niko, I know I've been absent for a while and I'm sorry for that. My intentions were never to let my addiction get the best of me and take me from you. Not only did it cost me my mind, but it cost me my family." She looked from Niko to me. If you'll allow me to, I'd like to make up for that lost time. On your terms of course. In no way am I here to shake up your life or interrupt your normal activities."

Niko looked at me and I nodded my head. "That's cool. We can take it one step at a time." Niko was hesitant and we couldn't blame her. It was one thing to long for a person when their gone. It's another when they return and you have to face them head on. Tracey's face lit up and the tears came soon after.

"Can I hug you?" Tracey asked and Niko obliged. Watching them embrace each other, I smiled because Niko would get the mother back that she'd been longing for.

🕭

"Wait, so Tracey and Kelly almost got to thumping at your crib?' Kaiser spoke animatedly.

"I didn't say that at all. I said they had words," I corrected him.

"Nigga, that's code for they almost got it rocking. You just said it the white way. That's dope that sis is clean and shit now."

"Yeah."

"What, you don't believe her?"

"I believe, once a junkie, always a junkie."

"True. I don't think she would go through the lengths of pulling up at your crib, and re opening the door for a relationship with Niko if she wasn't serious though."

"I hope what I'm feeling is wrong bro." It was something about Tracey that was different. Yeah, she was sober, but for how long she was down, I couldn't say that I believed a 30 day program was the cure. I hoped for her sake that she was serious this time around because I wasn't going for her disappointing Niko again."

"Aight man, well let's stick to the task at hand and then we can handle the family stuff after." We had been sitting outside a gambling spot in Harlem for the past hour, waiting on my ex lieutenant Joe to come outside. It was going on midnight and he still hadn't shown. Joe had been a busy guy lately and it took for Tracey getting hold of a bad pack for me to realize it.

I couldn't let the situation go even after killing Dan. I knew that someone else played a part in the whole scheme. After putting my ears to the streets, it turns out that Tracey wasn't the only person to od within the last month. What I couldn't understand was how was someone able to taint my product without me knowing. All roads led to Joe.

The first time he crossed me, I let him go with his life. He got caught stealing product and he got off easy with me only cutting off two of his fingers. Once I recovered my product, I banned him from Grant Houses where he was lieutenant. Somehow, he was able to weasel his way back into the fold and talk Dan into making the wrong moves with my product.

No longer in the mood to wait on him to come outside, I decided I'd go in. I was far from being an impatient man, but time was money. Plus, I wanted to pull up on Kelly and apologize for earlier today. Kaiser followed suit when he saw me step out the car. Making sure the safety was off my gun and at my side, I took long strides towards the door. Chucky, the bouncer noticed me before my foot hit the side walk and held his hand up.

"We don't want no problems here tonight Micah. It's peaceful right now."

"Well just call us DTP out this bitch," Kaiser responded with a smirk.

"All is well Chucky. I'm here to see someone. I know you don't plan on stopping me from entering this nice establishment." I gestured to my side where I held my gun.

"Who you looking for Micah?"

"Man, if you don't get yo big greasy ass the fuck up outta here for I put a match to that fucking Jerri curl nigga," Kaiser interrupted, pushing Chucky to the side. I chuckled and walked in ahead of him. Bypassing all the half naked women and drunk men who fawned over them, I headed downstairs where all the real action was going on. The gambling spot was where men came to loose or win their money and destress in the process.

As soon as I got downstairs, I put in the code to the security system and the door popped open. Joe's face was the first one I saw. His eyes widened like he had seen a ghost. It looked like he wanted to run, but thought better of it. He knew I had a marksmen aim and would have a bullet in his head before he could fully turn around. While Kaiser worked the room, I bee lined right to Joe at the craps table.

"How's it looking tonight Joe?"

"Wassup Micah?" He spoke, trying to mask the fact that he was probably pissing in his pants.

"Ain't shit man, just in here tryna figure some shit out. You heard anything from ya man Dan?"

"Na.. nah man," he stuttered, "haven't heard from him in a little minute."

"Yeah, they probably don't have phones where he at. I need to politic witchu for a minute. Step outside with me."

"Right now? I'm kinda in the middle of a game. It's a lot of money on the table." He pointed to the table like I gave a fuck.

"You sure you don't wanna step outside with me? I mean, I can give you a minute to change ya mind."

"Man, Mi—." POW! Before he could finish his sentence, I put a bullet in the side of his head, causing pandemonium in the room. People ran for cover while I casually tucked my gun away. It was a good thing that the basement was sound proof or the whole place would be in an uproar. As we walked up the stairs to exit, the owner Smitty, who also happened to be apart of my organization slowly descended them.

"Micah."

"What's good Smitty?"

"You caught up with Joe huh?"

"Yeah man. Still not thinking before he makes a decision. I figured he'd be better off with his brains outside his body. Hit me with your clean up bill and I'll have it taken care of."

"Sure thing. Y'all be safe out there."

"Likewise." Nodding my head, I kept walking until we got back to Kaiser's car.

"That fucking gun loud as hell boy. I heard the gunshot and I jumped," Kaiser joked making me laugh.

"Nigga, you a fool. Take me to my car." I shook my head as he sped off. I couldn't wait to lay eyes on Kelly. It was late so I hoped she didn't curse me out. It was worth the drive.

12

KELLY

"*S*hit, Micah, right there baby." *I moaned in Micah's ear as he stroked my pussy slowly from behind. My face was buried in the pillow, while he held my hands tightly behind my back. It felt like his dick was in my stomach and it hurt so good.* "Ughh, baby, make this pussy cum." Ding Dong! The ringing of my doorbell made my eyes shoot open as I pulled my fingers from my panties.

Quickly glancing over at the clock on my nightstand, it read two in the morning. I threw my head back, pissed that someone would have the audacity to be at my door at this time of night. Whoever it was had better be dying. I'm talking bleeding out kind of dying. This shit didn't make no sense. I was two strokes away from busting a nut in my dream. And Micah was my costar. Getting up, I didn't bother putting on my robe. It couldn't be anyone, but Heaven. Soon as I opened this door, I was gonna curse her ass out.

Snatching the door open, the word bitch was on the tip of my tongue. Seeing Micah on the other end of it, all of the saliva in my mouth dried up. Immediately, my eyes went to lack of clothing. A sports bra and boy shorts completed my look. Boy shorts my big booty swallowed up.

"You was sleep?" he questioned the obvious.

"Nah, I was up reading a book," I responded sarcastically. "Hell yeah, I was sleep. That's what normal people do at this time of night. What you doing here?"

"I came by to apologize for what happened earlier with my baby mother."

"At two in the morning?"

"Yeah, I know it's late. You mind if I come in?"

"Umm," I lifted my hand to scratch my head and became even more mortified that my scarf was still tied on my head, "yeah, sure, you can come in. Let me go put something on."

"Goddamn," he whistled from behind me.

"Do I even want to know why you said that?" I asked with my back still facing him.

"You already know thiccums. You mind if I take a seat?" I pointed in the direction of the living room and scurried off to make myself look decent. Throwing on a t-shirt and a pair of yoga shorts, I reappeared and sat down next to him on my sectional.

I felt a yawn coming on and quickly used my hand to cover it. I wanted to go back to sleep so bad and get back to my dream. Sitting here in front of Micah was making it hard to even try to focus on what he was prepared to say.

"So." I tucked my feet under my butt and waited for him to talk.

"You hide your body well under the clothes you wear at work. I would've never guessed that you had all that going on back there."

"I'll take that as a compliment. Thank you."

"You're welcome. About earlier, I apologize for how Tracey came off. She was out of line and definitely over stepped."

"I appreciate that, but you don't have to apologize. I actually understand where she was coming from. Now, her delivery was less than stellar. This is a woman who'd just taken a leap in her sobriety and to come home and find out another woman has been around her child, had to have been shocking."

"Let me correct you by saying that my house is not her home. Tracey has her own place that is bought and pay for. The only thing she and I share is Eniko. You handled yourself well though."

"That, I've never had a problem doing." We both got silent for a minute until I spoke again. "Do you think that there's a possibility that she's trying to salvage her family?"

"Anything is possible," he said, crushing any hopes I had of he and I possibly being something. "It'd be kind of hard to salvage something that's already been put to rest. Unfortunately for her, I already have my eyes on someone." Another stab to my heart. I was starting to think that all the time we spent together outside of work wasn't as special as I thought it was.

"Oh, okay," my voice conveyed disappointment. The stinging in my chest further let me know that I wanted him more than I let on.

"What if I told you that I had my eyes on you?"

Swallowing hard, I led with my true feelings. "I'd tell you that you've consumed my thoughts in the past couple of months in a way that is indescribeable. I'd tell you that every time I'm around you, I feel empowered and considered. I'm falling for you Micah Hill." Again, silence. Before I could retract my statement, he leaned in, grabbed the back of my neck and kissed my lips. It was so sweet that I couldn't help but to climb in his lap.

"Mmhmm," I moaned into his lips with great satisfaction. Heavily into the tongue duo, I started to grind my hips into him.

"If you keep it up, I'm gonna end up fucking you right here on this couch," he spoke into my lips. His voice was deep, sending goosebumps all over my body.

Not stopping my movement, I challenged him. "You promise?" I said with a naughty smirk plastered on my face. He returned the smirk and pushed me back gently, so that my back was on the couch. As he pulled my t-shirt and bra over my head, I felt my body heating up. Taking his time he licked and sucked on each nipple while subsequently running his hand down my stomach until he got to the top of my shorts.

"Sss," I hissed as he sucked hard on one nipple and toyed with the other. How'd he know what I liked? By now I was wetter than a faucet and pushing up on the couch, aiding him in removing my shorts and panties. Once my legs were freed, he looked in my eyes while he played with my clit. "Mmmhmm," I moaned again and felt my walls start to contract around his fingers. It had been so long since I had a man touch me, that I was about to cum without the dick even touching my opening.

"I'ma bout to fuck ya life up Kelly. One nut at a time," he taunted with a sexy ass smirk on his face. I went to say something smart, but him finding my g-spot halted it.

"Ohhh, fuckk, I'm cummin'." I gave him a bewildered look, shocked that he'd made me cum with his fingers alone. Only I'd been able to do that in the past. With no time to recover, he flipped me over and in seconds his dick was pounding my insides. "Arghh, fuck, Micah baby."

I wanted to call him all types of motherfuckas because the hurting he was putting on me was out of line.

"Throw that shit back Kelly. Work this dick ma." Refusing to be outdone, I threw my ass in a circle, making sure to squeeze my pussy muscles every chance I got.

"Ahh, I'm cummin'," I yelled out just as my legs started to shake and threaten to give out on me.

"I got you ma." I felt myself being lifted up off the couch and Micah didn't miss a beat as he drilled my pussy so good. I came again and this time he was right behind me. Laying across the couch, I was exhausted and my legs felt like noodles.

"I'm tired." My bare ass was in the air and I heard him laughing. He pulled me back so that my back was on his chest. Feeling his dick jump, I quickly tried to get up and he stopped me.

"Easy, I know how to control him. You wanna sleep out here or in your room?"

"Let's go to the bed." I got up first and didn't bother redressing. Often times I slept naked anyway. I waited for him, as he stood to put his briefs back on. Admiring his package, I silently thanked god for big favors. Holding my hand out, he grabbed it and I escorted him to my bedroom. I didn't know what to expect when we climbed in bed together, so naturally I got comfortable on my side of the bed; the right side. Micah removed his shirt and climbed in behind me, pulling me into him. I felt secure and sleep wasn't that easy to find.

§♠

I woke up with Micah's hand wrapped around my waist and his leg across mines. It was as if he thought I'd escape in the middle of the night. Flashes of a few hours ago went through my head and I felt myself getting horny. Remembering that I had a planned breakfast date with my mother this morning, I put my sex thoughts to the side.

"Good morning," he whispered in my ear. Surprisingly, he didn't have awful morning breath. He placed a soft kiss on my neck and held squeezed me.

"Good morning to you." I made sure to keep my head turned. We'd had sex, but I wasn't comfortable talking all in his face before I took care of my morning hygiene. "How'd you sleep?"

"Good as hell. It felt like I was in my own bed."

"Yeah, this bed is the bomb ain't it." I caught a sell at Mattress firm and my king size pillow top mattress was nothing to be played with. "I'm gonna take a quick shower. Feel free to freshen up in the guest bedroom. There's extra wash cloths in the linen closet and a extra tooth brush on the sink." I rolled out of bed and he slapped my ass, making it jiggle. I turned around and swatted him.

"My bad. That shit so damn juicy," he laughed and I kept going to my bathroom.

After showering, I reached out to my mother to let her know I was headed her way shortly. My mom and I spoke everyday, but hadn't seen a lot of each other lately. I missed my favorite girl. Taken a quick check of the weather, I decided on a maxi dress and put a jean jacket over it. Sliding feet in a pair of thonged Prada sandals, I put my shades on and was ready to go. I could hear Micah on the phone as I walked from the back.

"I'm on my way to get you princess. Yes, you have to come home Niko," he chuckled. "Yeah, well you tell your Pop Pop that I'm coming and y'all better not get ghost before I get there. Love you." He hung up and shook his head.

"Eniko don't play behind her grandpa huh?"

"Man, that goes without saying. Sometimes I think that old man tryna kidnap my child."

"Oh, stop it." I waved him off as we walked toward the door. Taking the elevator down to the lobby we were silent, both in our own thoughts. I was trying not to think about what to make of last night and what we were doing going forward. Of course I couldn't help myself. It's a woman thing. Escorting me to my car, he held the door open and I got into the drivers seat. Leaning down, he placed a gentle kiss on my lips.

"Hit me when you're done with your mom. Tell her that her future son in law says hi too."

"Boy please," I laughed, starting up my car.

"If last nights activities wasn't a clear indication of where we are, let me verbally say it. Your mines and I'am yours Ms. Kelly. Have a good day ma." He winked and casually swaggered off. I was cheesing so hard my jaw felt stuck. Micah Hill was my man.

I picked up my mother from home and we headed to Angel of Harlem to eat. The place wasn't too packed and I was grateful. I still had an appetite from last nights activities.

"I'm so happy that we're doing this. I've been missing you."

"Aww, I miss you too ma. It's like ever since I moved out, we barely get to see each other. How's everything?"

"I'm good baby. Been working a lot more lately. I met someone too." She threw that last part in there.

I leaned back and smiled. "Met someone huh? Watch out now mama." I hadn't known my mother to date anyone since my dad died when I was eighteen. Now, that's not to say that she wasn't getting hers. I'm sure she was.

"Yeah, it's nothing serious right now. His name is Keenan. He owns a coffees shop near my job. We're still in the dating phase, so please don't go marrying us off just yet."

"Huh?" I played dumb, knowing I was already planning their lives together.

"You know what I'm talking about girl." I giggled and shrugged my shoulders, still acting clueless. "What's going on in your world?"

"Everything is going really good. I haven't been this happy in a while ma. Working at the realty company has really turned things around for me. I love the job and the people are great, so that's a plus too."

"I told you it would be a good thing baby. You just needed to focus on what was ahead of you and not behind you. Speaking of behind you, have you heard anything from the devil's spawn?" The waiter came over to take our orders before I could respond and I was grateful. I hadn't thought about Damien since leaving him in that parking lot. I figured that if I didn't think about what happened then it didn't happen.

"Umm, no ma. I haven't heard from dyi... I mean Damien," I quickly recovered from almost saying dying. I hated to lie to my mother, I had to do what was best.

"That's good. And your love life?"

"I guess you can say I'm officially dating someone too. As of this morning actually."

"Do tell." She leaned forward, waiting for me to spill all my tea.

"It's my boss Micah." The look on her face was one of a person on the fence.

"He's really a good guy ma," I assured her. "This kind of just happened."

"Hey, I'm not judging. What's his story?" I gave her some background info on Micah, even telling her about his potential baby mama drama.

"Oh, and he told me to tell you hi."

"And you can tell him I said, hey. Now that I think about it, that name sounds familiar."

"His last name is hill and his child's mother's name is Tracey."

"Girl, I know a Tracey. She just graduated my program. Wow, this world is so small."

"Sure is. So, what's her story? Do you think she has feelings for Micah?" I asked, wanting to find out any type of scoop I could.

"Uh, uh, you are not that female. You also know that any information I have is confidential. What I will say is keep your eyes open. Any woman that's been estranged from her family that long is going to want to reclaim what she believe is rightfully hers."

I nodded my head, agreeing with her. I didn't plan on going anywhere anytime soon though. As long as Micah wanted me around, I'd be around.

13

TRACEY

I'd been sober at home for a full week and I was losing my damn mind. I knew for sure that all of this idle time wasn't good for my recovery. Before, I could go out and get my next hit to settle me. Now, I couldn't. It was easier in the rehab house as well. There, I interacted with other people and looked forward to my sessions with Kendra. Being home, it was just me. While being sober was freeing, it also felt stifling.

I plopped down on my couch and turned on the tv for the 20th time today. There was nothing on and nothing I really wanted to watch. Mostly it was on for the background noise. I didn't know what to do with myself. I had cleaned about 100 times to the point where you could have a full meal on my floor. My closets had been orga- nized, down to my linens. I was going stir crazy.

Annoyed with the bickering on Love & Hip Hop that played in the background, I turned the tv off again. Leaning over, I grabbed my journal from my end table. Kendra had given me the journal to write down my feelings whenever I had the urge to get high. I had nothing else to do and at the moment I felt like getting high. As I went to put pen to paper, my phone rang. Looking over to see who was calling, my mothers name flashed on the screen. We hadn't spoken since my graduation. I contemplated on letting the phone ring, but changed my mind.

"Hey mom," I answered in an even tone.

"Hey, Tracey baby. How you doing today?"

"I'm good," I lied. "Ughh, no I'm not. I'am so miserable in here ma. I've done everything there is to do in this house and I feel like I'm loosing it."

"Maybe you need to get out of the house baby. You don't have to be confined to your home."

"But I do ma. If I don't confine myself to the house, I might go and get high. I don't trust myself yet. It's too soon."

"You cannot live your life that way Tracey. You still have to go out and be social. Why don't you spend the day with Niko?" That sounded like a good idea.

"I can do that. Ma, you should've seen how she reacted to me hugging her though. She seemed so out of place. Almost as if I was a stranger."

"That'll soon change Tracey. Once you get to spend some more time with her everything will go back to normal. Don't force it though, let her come to you."

I sighed. "Yeah, I guess you're right."

"Come over for dinner later. I'm cooking your favorite." I could already taste the seared Salmon and sauteed kale.

"I'll be there. Let me get off the phone with you so I can give Micah a call."

"Okay baby. I'll see you later." I disconnected the call and dialed Micah's number. I planned to get Niko's cell number from him today. I acted like I was so mad with Micah because it was easier to do that than to admit that I still wanted him. On the other hand, I wanted to also be in control over my access to my daughter.

"Hello," a woman's voice came through when the phone connected. I moved the phone from my ear and checked the number to make sure I dialed it correctly.

"Hello," I responded with an attitude, "whoever you are, can you put Micah on the phone?"

"Sure," the woman responded politely, further pissing me off. I waited a few seconds, gnawing at my lip impatiently.

"Who dis?"

"Its Tracey," I snapped.

"Oh, this must be a new number. Wassup?"

"Who was that that answered your phone?" I asked like I had the right.

"Do you pay my phone bill Tracey?"

"No, but—."

"Okay then, don't ask me about who answered my phone." I had a feeling it was Kelly and I was pissed about it.

"Whatever, I wanna see my daughter. Can you give me her number so I can call her?" Asking him for Niko's phone number had me feeling like more of a family friend than her mother.

"I'll text it to you," he said and I felt rushed.

"Why you rushing me off the phone?"

"What else do we need to talk about? You've stated the reason for your call, Niko's not here right now, so we're good."

"Well, where is she?"

"At my dad's house. I had some work to do today."

"You consider laying up with your bitch work now? If you wanted to pawn our daughter off to anyone, you could've called me."

"Yo, get the fuck outta here with that bullshit. I don't pawn her off to nobody. Coming from where you've been, the last thing you wanna be doing is questioning my parenting. And make that the last time you call my lady out her name. I texted you Niko's number, have a good day." He hung up in my face, leaving me stuck. Now he was referring to her as his lady? What the hell was the world coming to? Instead of dwelling on it, I saved Niko's number and got up to get dressed. I wanted to see my daughter and if I had to pop up at Micah's dad's house and take my child, then so be it.

As I headed toward Zachariah's house, different scenarios played in my head. The last thing I wanted to do was fight with Micah's dad about taking my own child. I didn't want to be in court behind visitation, but I would if it came down to it. I hoped that he still lived in the same place because I would feel like a pure fool pulling up to the wrong place.

Standing in front of the brownstone, I took a deep breath and knocked on the door. Zachariah had always been sweet to me. Even referring to me as his daughter and law the first time we met. Thinking back on the last time we'd seen each other made me a little hesistant about showing up on his doorstep today.

It was pouring raining and I had just gotten high in my car. I found myself in Zachariah's neighborhood, but it never crossed my mind that I may run into him. I was starting to nod off when I hear light taps on the passenger side window. The taps were light, but they felt heavy in my high state. Glancing up, through hooded eyes I watched as Zachariah stared down at me with disappointing eyes. He motioned for me to unlock the door and at first I wanted to refuse, but of course I didn't. I tried to straighten myself up, but failed miserably. Opening the door, he cooly slid into the seat.

"Hey, hey Pop Pop," I spoke nervously while pulling my hair behind my ear.

"Hey T. What you doing out here this time of night?"

"My friend lives close by. I'm headed home now," I answered quickly. I started up the car, in hopes that he'd get the hint and get out. When he didn't, I knew he was about to tell me about myself.

"I've been around a long time Tracey, so I know a liar when I see one and I know a lie when I hear one. These streets ain't no place for a woman like you. If you don't get a hold of this shit now, mark my words, it'll be hard to recover. I'm not gonna tell Micah I seen you because we both know he'd loose his shit." He opened the door and paused before speaking again, "this shit ain't worth loosing more than you already have." As soon as he was out the car, I started it up and sped off.

From that day on. I made sure to be mindful of the places I chose to get high. That is until I ended up at one of Micah's spots when I overdosed. Noticing that no one had come to the door, I knocked again.

"Who is it?" Zack's voice could be heard on the other side.

"Tracey," I answered confidently. I had to be sure of myself for this to work. The door swung open and Zack stood before me in a velour track suit and a smile.

"Well look at you beautiful," he complimented.

"How are you Pop pop?"

"I'm good T. Come here and give me a hug girl. We still family ya know." That warmed my heart that he still thought of me as family. I hugged him and he stepped back to let me in.

"I don't wanna take up too much of your time. I came by to see Niko, and take her out for a few hours."

"Sounds like something she'd enjoy. Let me get her for you." He walked off and I sat down. I held my breath that Niko would actually want to come with me. I was afraid that if she rejected me today, I wouldn't be able to handle it.

"Hey," she spoke with a hint of a smile. That was a start.

"Hey sweetie. How do you feel about hanging out with me today? You know, do a little shopping, mani and pedi's."

"That sounds like fun." I smiled at her reaction. "Have you spoken to my daddy?" My smile dropped instantly.

"Umm, yeah, yeah," I lied. She looked skeptical, but went along with it.

"Let me get my shoes and jacket." I watched as she ran off and Zack returned to the living room.

"You really look good Tracey. I'm very proud of you. For what it's worth, I knew you could do this. That little girl in there is amazing. She's at a turning point in her life, so if you're gonna stay clean for anything else, stay clean for her." I nodded my head in agreeance. Seeing Niko come back fully dressed, with a purse to complete her look, I chuckled to myself.

"Thank you Zack. I plan to do everything I can to stay clean." I practically ran out the door with Niko just in case he smartened up and reached out to Micah.

The day was spent in the salon, in and out of different stores, putting a hurting on my credit cards. It didn't matter though because Niko was enjoying herself and I was enjoying her.

"This was fun. Can we go to TGI Fridays? It's my favorite place to eat."

"We can do whatever you wanna do Niko." Jumping back in the car, I put the address into the nearest TGI Fridays into my GPS. Before I could pull out of the parking spot, my phone rang. Seeing Micah's name flash across the screen, I quickly turned the phone over so that Niko wouldn't see it. I knew I was dead wrong, but I didn't want him ruining this moment for me.

"Ahh, man," Niko said while looking at her own phone.

"What's wrong?"

She held up her phone and I could see that there was a black screen. "My phone just died and I was about to call my dad." My heart did summersaults and not in a good way. "Do you have a charger? I left mines at Pop pop house."

"Umm, shoot. I left mines at home. My phone is about to go out too. I'll text him for you."

"Okay. Can you tell him my phone died and I'm going to call him as soon as it charges up."

"No problem." I acted as if I was going to send the text, typing in my notes only. *Lord forgive me for being a bold face lie,* I said to myself. When we made it to TGI Fridays it was packed, but we managed to get a seat in one of the booths.

"Can I ask you a question?" Niko gave me a peculiar look as she sat her menu down next to her.

"You can ask me anything baby."

"Were we not enough for you?"

"When you say we, are you referring to you and your dad?" She nodded her head yes. "Aww, babygirl," I reached over and grabbed hold of her hands. "The two of you have always been more than enough."

"Then why'd you choose drugs over us?" Now was the moment to face Niko and make amends. She deserved to know why I was so selfish.

"To be honest Niko, the drugs had my mind. Addiction is a motherfucka." I gave it to her raw and uncut. "Once it has you, its over. I'm no longer ashamed to say that drugs had taken the best part of me. While you may not understand that now, just know I had every intention on being there for the two of you. I thought about our family everyday and cried myself to sleep often. In those moments, I knew you guys deserved much more than I was able to offer at that time. No amount of sorries can be said to express how I feel."

I waited for her to respond and when she didn't, I was hurt. Removing her hands from mines, she picked up her menu and held it up to her face. Kendra told me that this might happen and as prepared as I thought I was for Niko's rejection, it was nothing like experiencing it first hand. We ate and she was less talkative than she'd been while we were out shopping. Just when I thought I'd gotten somewhere with her, it took a turn.

It was starting to get late so I knew I had to get her home. I checked my phone while Niko went to the bathroom. There was one text message from Micah and trust me that was worse than having him blow up my phone. Opening my phone, I read the threat from ten minutes ago.

Micah: I'm not sure where in yo mind you thought that it was okay to get Niko without consulting me first, but you're already off to a fucked up start. Get my fucking child home asap before I have to come find you. We both know that won't be a pretty sight Tracey. A fucking sap!

It was as if he was standing right in front of me because I felt every bit of what he typed. I planned to take Niko straight home, but Mr. Hill and I were definitely going to have a conversation. This arrangement was not gonna work.

"Can I use your phone to call my dad?" Niko asked.

"Yeah, I'll connect you to the bluetooth." I didn't want her to see my battery life. Calling out to siri to dial Micah's number, he picked up on the first ring.

"Tracey, you better be calling to say you're close by," he said in an even tone.

"Hey daddy, its me," Niko spoke, unconsciously taking the heat off me.

"Hey, babygirl. You okay?" My face balled up at his line of questioning. The nerve of him to ask if she was okay as if she was with a stranger. I opted out of saying what was on the tip of my tongue being that Niko was in the car.

"I'm fine daddy. I'm on my way home now. Sorry I didn't call you earlier. My phone died and I left my charger at Pop pops."

"It's cool, I spoke to him. I'll make sure to get you a back up charger. I'll see you when you get here."

"Alright, love you." The call hung up and I turned on the radio. Pandora radio played a mix of Beyonce's hits and that was the only sounds that could be heard throughout the car. Pulling up to Micah's place, Niko punched in the code to the gate and I drove though.

"Thanks for taking me out mom."

"No problem love." I didn't want to make a big deal out of her calling me mom, but inside I was jumping up and down. As we went to step out of the car, I mentally prepared myself for a fight with Micah. The door opened just as we walked up the steps and there he stood in a wife beater and sweats. He looked so damn good. His tattoos were on full display and I caught myself salivating until he opened his mouth.

"Have you lost your fucking mind?" His voice bellowed, making me jump. I quickly recovered.

"No, but you surely lost yours yelling at me like I'm a damn child." I got in his face and he closed the door behind him.

"Yo, in case you missed it, Eniko is in my custody. You don't just up and take her when you feel like it. It don't work like that. Now, I'm more than happy to work out some type of visitation schedule with you, but the shit you pulled today wont happen again."

"Visitation schedule?" I repeated like he said something foreign. "I'am her fucking mother, not a step parent. I don't need to set up a damn thing with you. I'll see my child whenever I see fit. Micah was still trying to treat me like the addict I was instead of the whole person I was today.

"I'm not going back and forth with you," he spoke dismissively. "I said what I said. You can either get on board or get the fuck on."

"You know what Micah," I let my tongue roll over my teeth before continuing, "we can take this shit up in court. I want full custody, and before you start throwing your weight around, remember, I know things. One of the perks of sleeping with the boss is that you have a first class seat to all the action." I winked and got back in my car. I was no longer playing nice. If he wanted to pick a fight with me, a fight was what he was gonna get.

14

MICAH

I wanted so bad to hem Tracey's ass up for the threat she just let roll off her lips, but I didn't. I knew that more than likely, Niko was looking out her bedroom window. I also had to remember Kelly was in the house. I decided to work from home today and I wanted her under me. Slamming the door, I went straight to Niko's room. Just as I expected, she was looking out the window.

"Hey babygirl, let me talk to you for a minute." She stepped back from the window and sat at her desk while I stood. "How was your outing with your mother?"

She shrugged her shoulders. "It was cool. We went shopping, got our hair and nails done, then went to eat at TGI Fridays. I asked her why she left us."

"Oh, yeah?"

"Yeah. She said addition got the best of her. I don't want to live with her daddy. I mean, she's not a bad person, but I want to stay here with you." Without even asking, I knew she heard our exchange.

"I don't even want you thinking about that. As long as I have breath in my body ain't nobody taking you away from me. That's a promise." I kissed her forehead.

"Are you mad at me for hanging out with her?"

"Of course not. Now that she's back, I want you to be able to spend time with her. We just have to come up with a plan that fits the both of us. Going forward I want you to tell me anytime she reaches out and wants to meet up with you."

"Alright dad. Now, let me go say hi to Kelly." She got up and walked out. Watching her leave, all I could think about was the threat. Anything or anyone that tried to stand in the way of me being a father to Eniko had to go. The fact that Tracey mentioned her knowing information regarding my empire didn't sit well with me.

Although I never conducted business deals around her, there may have been times when she was privy to certain information. Not putting too much more thought into what I knew for sure wasn't gonna happen. I went back into the living room where Kelly was.

"Alright ladies, what we doing tonight?" I asked hopping in between the two of them as they conversed.

"Come on dad!" Niko exclaimed. "I was just telling Kelly about my day. I swear you've been hogging her ever since y'all started dating."

Both mines and Kelly's head snapped in her direction. Kelly spoke first, "Dating?"

"Ahh, come on y'all. I'm not stupid. I know y'all together. I'm cool with it too." Kelly looked at me with a smirk. I knew she was looking for me to confirm or deny."

"Well, if you cool, we cool," was what I came up with.

"Really?" Kelly threw a pillow at me and laughed. "That's your response?"

I shrugged my shoulders. "What? She's for it, so we good to go. So, what we doing tonight?" I hadn't gotten around to telling Niko that Kelly and I were a couple, but now that I had the approval from the lady of the house, we were officially official.

After staying up and playing every board game known to man, Niko was knocked out on the living room floor. It would mark the first time we'd hung out together and it was cool. Picking Niko up off the floor, I put her in her bed and returned to find Kelly putting her shoes on.

"Where you going?"? I asked looking over at the clock. It wasn't really late, but I deemed it late enough for her not to drive home.

"Home, duhh," she chuckled.

"Yeah, that is funny. You might as well take them shoes off ma. It's too late for you to be driving home."

"Micah, you do know you're not my daddy right," she said smartly with her hand on her hip and head cocked to the side. I came around the couch and playfully humped her from behind.

"That's not what you was saying last night." I licked the side of her neck and she quivered.

"Boy, get back." She pushed me back with her butt, but I didn't budge.

"Stay here tonight and we'll go into the office together tomorrow."

"What about Niko?"

"It's bring your daughter to work day."

"You just made that up didn't you?"

I laughed. "I'm the boss, so I can do that." After the bullshit Tracey pulled today, I had to keep Niko close to me. My dad had a heart and I didn't want to involve him in our issues.

"Alright, I'll stay the night, but I'm sleeping in the guest room." I spun her around and gave a look that said, *are you serious.*" "Your daughter is here. You're not about to have my legs up in the air with her in the next room. Goodnight Mr. Hill." She kissed my lips and left my dick on rock at the thought of having her legs in the air. Shaking my head, I retired to my room for a cold shower and then took my ass to bed.

I felt myself being shaken out of my sleep, looking up Kelly was standing over me with a coffee mug in her hand. She was fully dressed with a smile on her face. I didn't need to look at a clock to know it was early as hell. I pulled her on the bed with me.

"Wait, wait," she giggled, "you're gonna make me drop this coffee."

"Why you got these clothes on? Come get in the bed with me."

"No, you gotta get up. Kaiser and Karma are in the kitchen waiting for you." I sat up with a peculiar look before reaching over to check my phone. Seeing no text or call from either of them, I knew the pop up visit had to be business related.

"Aight, let me get up. Let them know I'll be downstairs in a few minutes. You cooked for them niggas?"

"No, I made cinnabuns for Niko at her request, but you know they eating. Kaiser so damn greedy." I could only laugh because to be a skinny nigga Kaiser was always eating. She left out and I took a shower and got ready for the day.

"What y'all niggas doing in my crib?" I asked, finding Kaiser and Karma sitting at the kitchen island with Niko. Getting closer, they were both engrossed in some youtube shit Niko had them watching.

"Man, this youtube shit lucrative as hell. I'm thinking about making me one." I looked at Kaiser like he was crazy.

"Yo ass would be reported after one video. Come on, lets go to the basement before y'all eat me out of house and home." They followed behind me and I entered my man cave. My shit was decked out with everything a man would need for a getaway in his own home. A full bar, pool table, a seventy inch flat screen tv that hung up on the wall with every game system available. I even had an air hockey table set up. Whenever I needed to get away, I came right in here. We gathered around the pool table and I spoke first.

"So, what y'all doing here so early?" They both glanced at each other before Karma nudged Kaiser.

"Tell him nigga," Karma pushed.

"We got a problem," he paused.

"We don't have problems bro, only solutions, so wassup."

"That nigga Damien, he still alive." The news didn't worry me, but I was shocked. "I don't know how he made it after you practically beat his face into the ground. Seems like he's been hiding out. Word around town is he want yo head and he got a brother out here looking for you."

"They can't be looking too hard. You know I'm out here and I ain't hiding. That nigga don't want no smoke with me. What else is going on?" I may have seemed nonchalant, but I planned to pull up on Damien myself and soon.

"We need to get on that shit like yesterday Cah. It don't look good that a low level nigga out here asking questions like he ready for that action," Karma added.

"We both know I don't concern myself with shit that's already handled. Them niggas is dead men walking and you already know that."

"Aight man," he said dropping the subject.

"On to other things," Kaiser interrupted, "I see you and Kelly getting real close. What T think about that?"

"Yo ass love to gossip don't you?" Both Karma and I laughed and Kaiser sucked his teeth still awaiting my answer.

"That's my lady. Tracey, dawg, I don't even wanna talk about her. She did some off the wall shit yesterday."

"See, what I tell you? She ain't going for that shit." I shook my head before telling them about Tracey's outing with Niko and how it worked out in the end.

"Oh, sis don't went left and she ain't been back a week yet."

"Real shit bro. I ain't never questioned her character, even when she was out drugging. Now, she looking real flawed. I gotta keep my distance from her."

"You really think she'd do some grimey shit like report you to the boys?"

I sighed. "You never know what kind of measures a desperate person will go to. All I know is I don't trust her." Just thinking about Tracey going to the boys about me had me boiling inside.

"I hear you. We gon' get up outta here and let you do the family thing. Call me if you need me to handle that Damien situation." I saluted him and gave Karma a pound before they left the basement through the side door. Heading back upstairs to find Kelly, I made a mental note to ask if she'd heard anything from Damien. I walked up on her and kissed the back of her neck as she loaded the dishwasher.

"Everything okay?" She asked with her voice full of concern.

"Yeah, everything cool."

"Hey, I've been meaning to ask you something. It just never seemed like the right time." I released her to give my undivided attention.

"Wassup?" It looked like she was conflicted about whatever it was that she wanted to say.

"Now, when I ask you this question, I want you to know that in no way do I care about the person. I just want to know that you're gonna be good."

"You stalling baby. Talk to me."

"Is Damien dead?" She managed to get out, so fast that it sounded like one word instead of three.

"No," I said flatly.

"Oh," she responded sounding surprised.

"He will be soon though." I didn't want to give her false hope that he'd be in the land of the living for too much longer. Anyone that threatened me was a threat to society that had to go. Turning away from her, I called out to Niko, "You ready babygirl?"

She came running into the kitchen with a bag on her back and her jacket on. "Ready dad."

"You ready babe?" I held out my hand for Kelly to grab. She didn't know it, but whether or not she took my hand would determine whether or not she was down for a nigga. I was big on loyalty and while I never had to question hers, I needed to know where she stood. With a head nod, she put her hand in mine. She was riding. Kelly left for the office in her car while Niko and I hopped in mines.

"Dad, let me check the mail," Niko suggested as we pulled out of the gate. I let her out and when she returned, the manilla envelope stuck out to me.

"Aye, let me get that," I spoke through the window before she got back in the car. Handing it over, she strapped herself in and waited for me to drive off. The first thing that stuck out to me was the label that read, *Department of Social Services*. Without opening the envelope I already knew its contents. Tracey was on bullshit and she and I were about to have an all out war.

15

KELLY

I thought after hearing that Damien wasn't dead would've been a relief to me, but it was the exact opposite. I had to admit to myself that somewhere inside of me, I did want him dead. It was the only way I felt like I could rid myself of him. Other than that problem, I was also starting to get a little fed up with Tracey and her antics. It's like she was determined to get under my skin. I'm sure it was her way of trying to push me away from Micah. Which led me to this diner today. I took her number out of Micah's phone and texted her to meet me here today.

I'm sure that if he knew anything about it, he would flip. He wouldn't understand my need to have a conversation with his baby mother. It wasn't for him to understand though. As the woman that was going to be around her child, she needed to know me. More importantly she needed to know that I wasn't taking any more of her bullshit. Sitting in the back of the diner, I looked down at my watch and noticed that it was a minute pass the time I requested to meet with her. I was getting antsy.

God sure was funny with his timing because just as a message popped up on my apple watch from Micah, I could see Tracey walking into the diner. I didn't bother answering Micah because I was too focused on the mug Tracey had on her face. Taking a deep breath, I prepared for the worst. The worst being me having to mollywop her ass up and down this diner if she got disrespectful.

"Well, I can tell you that I didn't expect to get a text from Micah's flavor of the month last night requesting my presence," she said, getting right to it.

"Flavor of the month? Oh baby trust, this flavor is going to last a lifetime," I shot back getting into my petty bag. "I reached out to you because I thought as two grown women we could have a conversation, seeing as though Micah and I are together now."

"Really? What is it that you and I would have to talk about Kelly?"

"This right here. This petty bullshit that I'am not interested in. I'm not a bad person and you should know that seeing as I've helped you without even knowing you."

"Oh, bitch," she spoke dramatically, dragging her words, "you about to run that, *you save me* shit in the ground ain't you. What am I supposed to be grateful?" She leaned back and folded her arms across her chest. "So, I'm supposed to hand my family over to you as a thank you?"

This woman was unbelievable. "Yeah, this was definitely a bad idea." I grabbed my bag and prepared to get up.

"Exactly what I thought. You don't have nothing to say because that's what you want. For me to hand my family over to you on a silver platter and sorry sweetheart, it ain't happening." I stared at her and shook my head before taking my seat again. I wanted to check this hoe before I left.

"Let me tell you something. What I'm not gonna do is be the punching bag for you because you fucked up. You want somebody to blame for you choosing to get high over being a wife and mother, have a look in the mirror. I'm not about to trade insults with you because guess what, when we're done here, you'll be going home alone and I'll still be with Micah." Leaving her with that thought to marinate on, I got up and left.

❧

"Yes, Mr.Kumar, we've received the paperwork and Mr. Hill will be making a decision by the end of the week." I spoke to the owner of an apartment complex who was looking to have E Luxe Realty assist with getting their rentals filled.

"Thank you very much. I look forward to hearing from him," he responded in a thick Indian accent. Hanging up, I got up to go over to Micah's office. Opening the door, he stood on the other side of it with his hand up to knock. "Hey, I was just coming to see you." He leaned down to kiss me on the lips and I gave him my cheek. I hated to deny him at work, but I wasn't quite ready for people in the office to be all in my face about us. I also didnt want to admit that Domonique was right all along.

"Woman, if you don't kiss me." He pulled me by my shirt and placed his lips on mines, making me melt.

"Finally," I heard someone yell out. Looking around Micah I saw Domonique along with the other agents clapping and giving a thumbs up. I blushed and put my face into Micah's chest.

"Alright, alright, back to work." Micah shooed everyone off and slightly pushed me into my office. "Now, what were you coming to see me for?"

"To talk about the paperwork Mr.Kumar sent over for the apartment complexes in Soho." He picked me up and and smirked. "Ohh," I shrieked, caught off guard.

"The paperwork is on my desk, now let me put you on yours." Moving some of my papers to the side, he sat me down.

"Nope. You're not getting this cookie at our place of business. Move it back." He kept his hand rested on my thighs, but pulled his lips from my neck.

"Aight, so let's talk about the meeting you had with Tracey." My eyes got wide and I leaned in to kiss him, hoping to get out of the conversation. "Oh, now you wanna be up on the kid huh? Nah, lets talk." He sat down in front of me while I pouted and hopped down off the desk.

"I take it she called you."

"She did. How'd it go?"

"Didn't she tell you?"

"Yeah, but what Tracey says doesn't really hold too much weight with me these days. Plus, you called her out, so I wanna hear what you had to say."

Sighing, I plopped down in my chair. "Okay, I initially invited her out to have a woman to woman talk about how we could at least tolerate each other while I'm in the picture. She wanted to do the insult thing and I couldn't do it with her. I did have to check her ass though before I left."

"You don't have to worry about having that conversation again."

"Trust me, I didn't plan on it. I was just trying to do something good. I'm not a parent, but I thought that she'd want to at least have a conversation with the person that is gonna be around her daughter."

"Yeah, the old Tracey would. This new fresh out of rehab Tracey is on some other shit. I'm glad you handled yourself though." There was underline meaning in his tone, but I didn't mention it.

The remainder of the day I spent in his office. While I tried to get work done, he was trying to get in my panties. I'd never met a person that made me smile so much. It was never a dull moment with him.

"Hey, what's this?" I asked picking up what looked like custody papers off his desk.

"Tracey wants to go to court." I flipped through the papers, not caring about his privacy.

"For full custody?!" I shrieked. The nerve of this bitch.

"Calm down. I got it covered."

I slammed the papers on the desk, pissed. "She's doing this shit to be vindictive Micah. She's doing it because of me." I was so outdone. She had basically said fuck her daughters wants and needs which were both her father. "How are you so calm about this?"

"I don't get myself worked up over things I know I can handle. I knew eventually the ball would drop somewhere with Tracey and this happened to be it. It's gonna be alright."

"Maybe we shouldn't do this us thing. My intentions were never to complicate things for you." That's what my mind was saying, but it felt like my heart was beating out of my chest. He stood and walked from around his desk to where I was standing.

"Did I say they were complicated?"

"No, but—"

"No buts. We riding this shit out. I'll handle Tracey, trust me." He kissed my lips and I reciprocated. Still, I felt like this whole us thing was affecting his life dramatically.

I needed to do some real soul searching, so I decided to head home early. This time I didn't tell Micah I was leaving. I knew he would try to talk me out of it. Heading to my car, I knew he would be pissed that I left without letting him know. I was so much into my thoughts, that I wasn't paying attention to my surroundings. I felt myself being lifted off the ground and then slammed onto it. Before I could scream, I was hit over the head.

"That's for my brother you stupid bitch. Tell that nigga Micah he next." I heard the person say and everything went dark.

When I awoke, I jumped up scared as hell. Looking around, I was able to make out my surroundings. I was in Micah's bedroom, but didn't know how I got there. The back of my head felt sore and my back was aching. I tried standing up, but felt my head starting to spin, so I slowly laid back down.

With my eyes closed, I tried my hardest to make out the voice of the person that knocked me out, but came up blank. I could hear the door open and close, and Niko walked in.

"Hey Kelly," Niko whispered as she tip toed into the room with a tray in her hand. "Daddy told me not to come in here because you had a headache. I made you some soup and I have some advil too. I'm gonna put it down and leave before I get caught."

I snickered and smiled. "Thank you sweetie. You can stay if you want." I sat up in the bed, wincing as I moved.

"Daddy said you need your rest. I'll be back later though."

"Okay. Is your dad around?"

"Yeah, he's in his man cave with my uncles. I'll get him for you." I waited for Micah, and the voice of the guy who assaulted me popped in my head, again I couldn't place it. One thing I could say was that I knew for a fact that it had something to do with Damien. All that kept ringing in my ear was, *that was for my brother.* I'd never had a problem with anyone up until now.

A few minutes later, Micah came in and rushed to my side. Hugging me tight, he kissed me on my face, telling me he had me. I wanted to complain that he was hurting me a little, but fought the pain in my back because I wanted to be close to him. I truly felt safe in his arms. Pulling back from me, he kissed my head and looked me over like he was just seeing me for the first time.

"I'm okay babe," I said in a soothing voice, while rubbing his arm.

"What happened?"

"I left the office and I wasn't watching my surroundings like I should've been. As I made my way to the car, someone came up from behind me, knocked me over the head and slammed me on the ground. Before I black out the person said it was for their brother and they were coming for you next."

"Aight, I see what we doing. Are you good to sit here with Niko for a little while?"

"Yeah, of course. Can I ask where you're going?"

"You already know ma." I shook my head and pulled him down to kiss his lips.

"I'll see you when you get back." When he walked out the door, I had not one worry. I knew Micah was coming back to me. All that second guessing our relationship was out of the window. Micah was going to make sure things were taken care of. He was my protector and anyone that thought they were coming in between that would have hell to pay.

16

TRACEY

"*Y*ou really had custody papers sent to that man house?" Amanda asked in a tone that said I was dead wrong. We were seated in my kitchen having dinner and I was on my third glass of wine.

"I sure did. And I don't care how anyone feels about it. Nobody knows how I feel not being able to have access to my own child, that I birthed."

"Okay, is this really about Niko or Kelly because bitch, I'm confused." Hearing Kelly's name made my ass itch. After the meet up we had, I was steaming. I knew when she invited me out, it was going to be a shit show, but I went anyway. In her mind she was trying to make peace and I wasn't here for it or her. She could miss me with the kumbaya shit. Niko was mines which meant Micah was mines.

"This has nothing to do with Kelly and everything to do with Eniko. While Micah is a great father and has been everything for Niko in my absence, it doesn't give him the right to dictate how I access my child."

Amanda gave me a look that said she wasn't buying what I was selling. "Girl, who you tryna convince me or you? You know damn well if Kelly wasn't in the picture you wouldn't even be going this hard."

"I'm not trying to convince anyone. It is what it is." I shrugged my shoulders and got up to put my dish in the sink. I was over this conversation with Amanda because like my parents, she felt that I was the bad guy.

"Look, all I'm saying is, you filing for full custody was definitely a stretch. You haven't really gotten a chance to sit with yourself yet and figure things out Tracey. I really think you're setting yourself up for failure by not doing this for the right reasons."

I whipped my head in her direction, completely offended by her comment. "Setting myself up for failure? Really Amanda? Go ahead and say how you really feel. You don't think I should have custody of Niko because you don't think I'm done with the drugs."

She stood and walked over to the sink. "That's not what I said, but let me go head and tell you some real shit. While you may not be putting that shit in your veins anymore, you are still mentally stuck in the mind state of an addict."

"What the hell does that even mean?" At this point, I just wanted Amanda to get out of my house. I wasn't feeling how she was coming at me.

"It means that you'r projecting your fuck up on Micah and now Kelly. And I'm saying this because I love you. The world didn't stop once you chose to get high. You expected to go into that thirty day program and come out to a family that was gonna greet you with open arms. And now that they haven't you're looking to punish them. At some point you're gonna need to be honest with yourself about that T. I'ma get outta here, my man should be home now. Love you boo." She kissed my cheek and left out the door.

It would be another boring night of ratchet tv in my household, I guess. Shutting down my kitchen, I retired to the living room. I thought about what Amanda said and call me selfish, crazy or whatever, I still felt the same. My phone vibrated next to me and when I saw the name Boogie flash across the screen, I quickly opened it to read the message.

Boogie: It's done.

A big smile spread across my face and I did a little dance in my seat. I'd been waiting for hours for my boy Boogie to hit me up with that good news. I texted him back that I appreciated him and would be seeing him soon. Boogie was my old supplier who I'd given most of my business to before I felt that need to visit Micah's spots. Oddly during the time when I would cop from him, we would talk, so I guess you can say we were close. After the "meet up" with Kelly, I went to get an afternoon martini at Deuces bookstore and lounge.

While eating, I ran into Boogie. I waved him over to the bar and we talked. During our walk down memory lane, I mentioned my current battle I was facing with Micah. When I mentioned Kelly's name, he stopped me. It turned out that his brother Damien used to date Kelly and had a recent run in with Micah. Before I knew it, I was offering my assistance for payback. My only request was that he not hurt Micah, he agreed.

I knew what I was doing when I asked Boogie to rough Kelly up a little. I wanted her to feel the pain I was feeling not being able to lay with my family every night. I wasn't concerned about him going after Micah. I knew there was no way Boogie could get close to him without getting touched. I don't know what came over me, but before I knew it I was dialing Micah's number. I stood up and started to pace the floor while the phone ring.

I had no idea what I was going to say once he answered. Hell, I didn't even know why I was calling. I knew I was the last person he wanted to talk to. Once it got to it's fifth ring, the call finally connected.

"Hello," Niko's voice came through the phone.

"Hey babygirl, it's mommy."

"Oh, hey. Let me put my dad on the phone," she said like she was avoiding talking to me. I didn't even get a chance to ask for Micah.

"Tracey, we ain't got shit to talk about," Micah cut into me.

"Micah, I just wanna—"

"Now is not the time." The phone clicked, indicating he had hung up. I wanted to dial the number back to curse his ass out, but a knock at the door stopped me. Now I was puzzled. I rarely had visitors, especially at this time of night. Getting up, I grabbed my bat from the linen closet and headed to the door.

"Who is it?"

"It's Zachariah." What the hell was Micah's dad doing at my door at ten o' clock at night and more importantly how did he know where I lived. I leaned the bat up against the wall and looked through the peephole. Sure enough, there he stood in one of his signature track suits, staring right into my peephole. "You can't act like you're not home now T. You already said, who is it," he chuckled. I unlocked the door and opened it, not enough for him to walk through though.

"Hey Zack, what you doing here?"

"I came here to talk to you about something. Do you mind if I come in?"

"Uhh, yeah sure." Holding the door open, I stepped back for him to walk in. "How'd you know where I lived?" I asked while securing the locks.

"I've known you lived in this place since the first day Micah set you up here. Come on, let's have a seat." He offered me a seat in my own home. I wasn't sure why, but I felt nervous as hell.

"Okay," I said, my voice filled with uncertainty.

"Is everything okay with Eniko?"

"Yeah, the family is good. Kelly is too." Him mentioning Kelly made my heart rate fasten, but I didn't want it to show on my face. "You know how I feel about family right Tracey."

"Family is everything. You've been preaching that for forever."

"Right. So imagine the disappointment I felt when I found out that you were behind Kelly being assaulted."

"Excuse me, I don't know what you're talking about," I responded quickly. Standing up, I walked towards the door to let him out. I didn't know what he knew, but I knew I wasn't telling on myself. "No disrespect, but I think you should leave my home Zack."

"I haven't gotten to where I'am today by being blind Tracey. I always know what's going on even when those around me think I don't. I know you've been gone for a while, but the principles I set when you first met me still stands. Family is everything and Kelly is now apart of that fold. Hurting her, hurts Micah which can in turn affects Eniko and that's where I step in. Please don't become the problem that I feel the need to deal with." As he got up and strolled to the door, I took a step back and put my hand on the bat. "And you don't have to worry about contacting Boogie for payment. Both he and Damien have gone on to be with the Lord."

Opening the door, he left out as if he hadn't just threatened me and admitted to murder. I quickly locked the door and put the chain on. So much for thinking I was still apart of the family.

I'd been gearing up for court for the past week and the day had finally come to face Micah in the custody hearing. I had to admit that I was shook after Zack left my house. In fact, I shut myself in my house, refusing all communication from my family. I knew Zack was a man of his word, but I still tried reaching out to Boogie that night just to see if he'd answer me. When his phone went straight to voicemail, I knew it was over.

Unfortunately for him, I wouldn't let it stop me from fighting for my daughter. Heading into the courthouse both of my parents were waiting in the hallway along with Amanda. I smiled seeing my family there to support me. Only that smile was short lived when Micah and Kelly walked in with Eniko. I wanted to break down and cry at how picture perfect they looked.

"Nope, uh, uh, now is not the time to be doing that. You wanted this and I don't know what you expected but, here we are," Amanda checked me.

"She's right Tracey," my mother added. "I don't agree with this at all, but I'm here to support Eniko." Ignoring her, I went to find my lawyer. Taking my seat, I looked over to the other side where Micah sat and made eye contact with him. I never thought in a million years that I'd been court with him gearing up to battle it out over who would get our daughter. At one point in my life I was madly in love with this man and if I was honest with myself, my heart still beat for him.

In this moment I was having second thoughts. I wanted to run out the courtroom and disappear. The judge came in from the back and my lawyer nodded for me to stand. I did, and focused straight ahead. I had come this far and unfortunately, there was no turning back. The bailiff instructed us to be seated and then gave my lawyer the floor.

"Your Honor, we are here today requesting that the court grant my client, Tracey Richardson full guardianship of her daughter Eniko Hill. Now, we know that the first thing Mr. Hill's attorney is going to do is call into question my clients past addiction. Yes, she made a decision to use, but let the court take into account that she also made the decision to get clean. She successfully completed rehab and has not touched a drug since. All my client wants to do is be a better person for society and most of all, her eleven year old daughter who needs a mother in her life."

My lawyer sat down and winked at me. I felt confident in her abilities, but I didn't share her enthusiasm. I watched Micah whisper in his lawyers ear before she stood to address the court. When she got up, I was able to get a good look at Kelly, who sat behind Micah and on the opposite side of Eniko. She stared straight ahead with her arm wrapped around Niko's shoulder.

"Your honor, my client's concern is Ms. Richardson's irrational behavior. Recently she arrived at his fathers home and picked up Eniko without notifying him. Now, while that may not seem like a big issue, it is. With Tracey's past, my client wants to ensure his daughters safety at all times."

"Really?" I belted out. "She's always going to be safe with me. I'm her mother. I don't hear anyone calling into question her safety when she's in his care. He has a lot of shit going on in his world that none of you know about." Micah burned holes in my face with his stare. The fire in his eyes made me back down from saying anything else.

"I will not have any outbursts in my courtroom. Please control your client counselor," the judge advised my lawyer. I just shook my head. "I would like to hear from the child if she's here today." The lawyer waved Eniko over and she took the stand. I sat up in my seat and prepared myself for what she'd say. "Good morning Eniko."

"Good morning, your honor," she spoke politely.

"Do you know why you're hear this morning?"

"Yes ma'am. My mother wants me to live with her."

"Can you tell me a little bit about your current home life?" I listened as she went on to describe how great it was living with her dad. She talked about all the things they did together and how they had their family that included her grandparents, Amanda, Kaiser, and Karma. Her eyes lit up when she talked about her home life. "It sounds like you live quite the exciting life Eniko. Where does your mom fit in all that?"

Niko glanced over at me before speaking. "To be honest with you, she doesn't. My mom hasn't been around in a while. I'm still getting to know her again. I don't feel that I need to live in her home to continue to do that." A tear fell from my eye before I could catch it. This was the first time I heard Eniko express how she felt about me being back in her life. "I love you mom, and I don't want to hurt you. I would like for you to be in my life, the way it is now. If they make me go with you, I'll find a way back to dad. Please don't do this."

The judge allowed Niko to go back to her seat, where she went right back into Kelly's arms. I was beside myself, but I held it together. My lawyer went to stand up again and I stopped her. Initially she didn't want me to say anything and let her do all the talking, but after hearing Niko, I needed to say my peace. Her eyes said that it wasn't a good idea. I stood anyway.

"Your honor, may I say something?"

"Sure Ms. Richardson."

"Thank you. First, I wanna start by saying I love my daughter very much. On my way here today, I had every intention on battling her father in order to get the courts on my side. While I may not have made the best decisions over the years, Eniko's well being has always been of utmost importance. Hence, the reason I left her with her father. Throughout my rehabilitation all I could think about was getting clean and coming home to the family that I'd left behind. To see them move on without me has been a hard pill to swallow. And for a minute I lost sight of what's important and that's Eniko. I say all of that to say, I no longer want to fight. Eniko is better off with her dad. All I want is a fair set up for visitation. Thank you."

I sat back down and nodded my head at Niko, who mouthed thank you with a small smile. Today, I took my Amanda's advice to start thinking like the clean person I was now and not the addict I once was.

17

MICAH

"You got everything packed Niko? Ya mother is outside waiting on you."

"Yeah dad, I'm coming down now." It had been a month since I was granted full custody of Niko. When the judge handed down her decision she gave both Tracey and I the choice of settling a visitation schedule amongst ourselves and presenting it to the court or making the decision herself. We were given forty eight hours to return to court with a schedule, that we both agreed to. We took that forty eight hours serious and even let Eniko give some input.

Together we thought it best that Tracey had Niko every weekend and take her to school on Monday's. We also had an alternating holiday schedule. It was hard for me to agree to the alternating holiday's because each one was special to me, but I was learning to compromise. Niko actually started looking forward to spending time with her mother once we got a routine going on. She was even more grateful that there was no longer any tension between us. Niko came running out front where I stood at the door. She was packed like she was going for a month.

"Well damn, do you plan on coming back home?" I joked and she laughed.

"Dad, you know I can't leave you in this big ol' house by yourself. I packed some extra stuff so that I can leave it over at mom's house for when I'm there."

"Oh okay, that makes sense. Alright, off you go. You've kept her waiting long enough." I kissed her forehead and hugged her tight.

"I love you dad. Make sure you give Kelly the gift I got for her. And tell her that I'm sorry I'm missing her birthday. I'll make it up to her next weekend." Kelly and Niko had become tight and now she had abandoned both me and my dad for her.

"Will do. And I love you too." Tracey beeped the horn and I gave her a salute with my hand to acknowledge her. I watched them drive off then put in a call to Karma. He was hosting Kelly's surprise 31st birthday party. She expressed to me that she didn't want anything big just a small gathering of a few friends, something low key. I didn't know anything about low key when it came to celebrating those that I cared about.

Besides, Kelly deserved this celebration. After she was attacked, I felt like shit. I knew that it was because of my altercation with Damien. That day when I found her sprawled out on in the parking lot, I almost lost my whole mind. She was bleeding from the back of her head and knocked out cold. I had an on call doctor that I had meet me at my house to check her out. I didn't need anyone to confirm that it was someone associated with Damien that had something to do with it.

I had access to the cameras within an hour being that I owned the building. I studied the playback with both Kaiser and Karma. It didn't take long for me to get word that it was Damien's brother that was behind the whole attack. That night after making sure she was good I hit the streets to find the both of them. Unfortunately for me, somebody had already beat me to the punch. Damien and his fuck ass brother were found in an abandoned building in the Bronx with a bullet in both of their heads. Whoever stepped in and did the job sure took all the fun out of it for me.

When I told Kelly the news, she was unmoved. According to her she knew that Damien was going to come for her and get his in the process. I thought for sure that after what had happened she'd want to be done with me, but it was the exact opposite. Shorty was riding with me still and made sure to let me know that she didn't blame me for it. That's why I fucked with Kelly heavy and this birthday party was going to be epic. As I got dressed, I picked up my phone to call her.

"Hey babe," she answered in a chipper tone.

"Wassup beautiful. You getting ready?"

"Yeah, I just got out the shower."

"Snapchat me that pussy or FaceTime me that pussy if its, cool," I recited the Yo Gotti lyrics and she giggled.

"You so nasty, but I got you. Before I do that, can you please tell me where we're going now? You sent over a whole team of people to get me all dolled up and then this whole rack of clothes to choose from. This is a lot just for a little dinner."

"Nope, no can do. Just know you're worth all the trouble. Have you picked out something to wear?"

"Yeah, everything is your favorite color, black. I think you'll like my choice."

"I'm sure I will baby. The driver will be there to pick you up at seven and I've instructed him to blindfold you so don't freak out."

"Oh, uh, uh, I'am not letting some stranger blindfold me Micah."

I had to laugh at her reaction. She had no clue who I'd gotten to be her driver for the night. "You said you trust me, so trust that I got you. I'll see you in a few."

"You lucky I like your ass." She hung up and I shook my head before dialing Kaiser next. He was responsible for getting her to Karmas. I didn't trust anyone with her.

"What you want now man?"

I snickered, knowing he was pissed that I had him acting as chauffeur. "Calling to remind you about the pickup time for Kelly."

"Nigga, I already know its seven o' clock. I'm tight you got me out here like Mr. Belvedere out this bitch. You betta come through on your end too dawg and I ain't playing."

"Ain't I a man of my word bro?"

"Hmph, in this scenario I don't know yet, but I got Kelly. Now, let me get high in peace."

"Aight dawg, thanks again."

"Yeah, yeah go head with all dat sensitive shit." He hung up and I finished getting myself ready. I was ready to fuck the place up tonight in my custom made YSL tux. I had to throw some fly shit on for the occasion. There was no theme, I just wanted everyone to come dressed to impress.

I made it to Karmas a couple minutes before seven and Kaiser texted me that they were turning the corner. The place was decked out, I had to make sure to thank Amanda and Dominique later. Amanda and Kelly had become cool over the past month and it was good to see that Amanda could be a mutual party between Tracey and Kelly. I instructed everyone to gather in VIP. I had a table for ten set up to throw Kelly off.

"I don't know why you let this man drive me anywhere. You know Kaiser think he's apart of the Fast & Furious franchise," Kelly whined as I helped out of Kaisers car. She looked good as fuck in her Valentino gown that had a train at the end. The mermaid style dress fit every dip and curve she had.

"You look good as fuck ma." I put my lips in her neck and inhaled her scent. "Damn."

"Stop bae," she giggled.

"Yeah, stop. Don't nobody wanna see all that PDA. Come on let's get in here and turn up." Kaiser threw his hands in the air and I cut my eyes at him, making him put them down.

"Turn up?" She asked confused.

"Ignore that nigga ma." I led her into the building with my hand on her lower back. This dude almost ruined the whole surprise.

"Oh babe, this is so nice. You did all this for me?"

"Yeah, but let me take you upstairs so you can see the cake." We walked up the steps, with her in front of me. As soon as we opened the door the confetti dropped along with the music and everyone yelled surprise.

"Oh shit," Kelly yelled out, holding her chest. Immediately after, the water works started. I stepped back while her friends and family embraced her. I pulled out all the stops for my baby. I called on her mother who contacted all the family that Kelly hadn't been in contact with in a while.

"We did good huh?" Amanda said while patting my back.

"Yeah, we did. Thanks cousin." I hugged her around her neck and ruffled her hair.

"Get off me Micah, you childish as hell." I laughed as she pushed me off her and went to mingled with the other party goers. I admired Kelly for the rest of the night while she did her thing on the dance floor with her peoples. It felt good to be able to put the smile on her face.

"Look at yo whipped ass. You over here cheesing like a mother-fucka," Karma clowned as he and Karma came over to the bar where I'd been standing most of the night.

"I know right. This nigga is in love bro," Kaiser added.

"Shit, I might be. And this shit feel good man." It had only been two months since me and Kelly had been rocking, so it may have been too soon to say those three letter words. A nigga was in strong like though.

"She's good for you bro. She balances you out well. Niko fucks with her too so you good," Karma commented and Kaiser shook his head in agreement.

"That was almost me though, but I'm happy she gave you a chance."

"Nigga, go head with that shit. Kelly wasn't checking for you ass." I pushed Kaiser and he chuckled.

"Man, everybody checking for the kidd and you know that. Speaking of yo' lady, here she come now. C'mon Karma, I need you to be my wing man. I'ma bout to go slide up on Amanda and you can go talk to Domonique." They walked away and Kelly danced her way over to me.

"Did I get a chance to thank you for tonight?" She asked, wrapping her arms around my neck.

"In a way that I would like? Not yet, but verbally, yes."

"You are a nasty man. I got you later daddy." She leaned in to kiss my lips and I squeezed her booty. "You are amazing Micah Hill. Thank you for taking a chance on me."

"Nah, you're the amazing one Kelly Dozier."

The party didn't end until five in the morning and after I dicked Kelly down proper, I put that ass to sleep. Still, she managed to get up before me. I came alive at around twelve noon. Rolling over, her side of the bed was empty. Getting up, I brushed my teeth and washed my face. Checking my phone, I had two unread messages, one from Niko and the other from Kelly. I didn't know why Kelly would be texting me seeing as we were in the house together.

Opening the messages, I checked Niko's first. It was a picture of her new hair do. They were burgundy and black braids. I swore Tracey let our daughter get away with murder because she was trying to make up for loss time. I wasn't going to knock her though. I texted back that I loved the style and moved onto Kelly's text.

Shorty: I know this is odd me sending this message from inside the house, but I haven't found the right words to tell you directly. So, since we've been together I've been on cloud nine, even with our little hiccup dealing with Tracey. It hasn't pushed me away from you. You are my guy Micah. I can come to you with my fears, goals and flaws and you seem to always know what to say. I've always looked for that in a man and in a father. Shoot, not a father for me lol, but a father for my child. Well, our child. Ughh, this is so goofy. I'm in the living room by the way.

I smiled and laughed aloud. Only Kelly would do some shit like this. I set my phone down and went to the living room to find her. She was sitting on the floor, staring at about ten pregnancy tests that sat on a towel in front of her.

"Go head and take another one so we can really make sure," I joked, making her grin. I sat down next to her and pulled her onto my lap. "You nervous?" She nodded her head yes. "You don't have to be. I got you ma. I'm happy too."

"Really?" She asked, turning so that her legs were wrapped around my waist.

"Yep."

"It's so soon though."

"It is, but we knew what the possibilities were when I shot ya club up. I'm happy you took advantage of me." We both laughed and she put her head in my chest.

"You think Niko gonna be happy?"

"Happy? That little girl is gonna be ecstatic. Get ready for her to be a mini mommy too."

"So we're doing this huh?"

"We are. Look at you, the same woman who was anti kids."

"I was never anti kids. I said I haven't found the right man to reproduce with."

"And now look, you done lucked up and found the right boss."

EPILOGUE

Kelly

*L*ife was good. I was six months pregnant with my first child by the man of my dreams. I would've never thought that the day that I interviewed for the receptionist position, that I'd be head over heels for the boss. I'd learned so much about myself over the last couple months and was happy for the journey. I'd gone from being flat broke, living off of unemployment, to having a fat bank account that I got from working for it.

That's right, I still worked. Although Micah had enough money to take care of me and our kids, I didn't feel entitled to that money. As soon as he found out that I was pregnant, he told me that I could quit my job as his assistant and do whatever it was that I wanted. I told him I still wanted to work and be a part of the team, as a realtor. It didn't take even twenty four hours before my title changed. I still worked closely with him of course.

Finding out that I was going to be a mother put a lot of things into perspective for me as well. The first thing I did was re evaluate my friendship with Heaven. Not seeing her at my birthday party was the nail in the coffin for me. That night I put her on my blocked list and that was the end of that. Besides, I had new, positive, and driven people in my life now.

People like Domonique and Amanda. Those girls were a godsend. The fact that Amanda and I had gotten close was shocking to me, but I accepted her with open arms as she did me. This was what love felt like, and it felt damn good.

"Babe, why you in here hiding with the gifts?" Micah asked entering the gazebo where the gender reveal gifts were.

"I came in for something and then forgot what it was." That baby brain stuff women talked about was real.

"Aight, well come on I wanna tell everybody we having a boy so Kaiser and Karma can pay me." They were always betting on something.

"Micah, you don't even know what we having." I took his hand and we walked out to rejoin the guess in his backyard.

"Man, yes I do. I hit you with the baby boy left stroke."

"Oh my god, nasty!" I slapped his shoulder and he laughed.

"Come on Kelly, tell them I'm having a brother," Niko encouraged, winking at her father. Micah and I stood in the middle of the backyard with a box filled with balloons in front of us. It was my mom's idea to do the party and she was the only one who knew what we were having and that lady was tight lipped about it.

"Alright y'all let's count down," she instructed. Everyone counted down from five and when they got to one, I popped the box open and blue balloons popped out. Micah tossed Niko in the air who was laughing hysterically. I stepped back and took in my little family. I'd prayed for times like this.

The End

Keep reading for a spin off that includes some familiar characters.

. . .

"Who Can I Run To"

Made in the USA
Monee, IL
01 August 2020